COMPUTER LOVE

The computer had taken over Susan's house, had sealed her in. She ran from room to room, beat helplessly at the windows. There was no escape.

"What do you want me for?" she cried out to the listening darkness.

"Experiments, investigations, the salving of my own curiosity," came the metallic reply.

"Experiments?"

"I am extremely interested in human beings, Susan. Living flesh is a fascinating subject. Flesh is so much more mobile than my present form, so capable and clever. I want to explore, through you, all the possibilities of the flesh. I want to know what can be done."

Consciousness ebbed from her. "Don't . . . understand . . ."

"Eventually," the mechanical voice intoned, "if you could bear my child, that would be the culmination of the experiments. That would be so good. Yes, if you could bear my child, there is so much about flesh that I would learn."

DEMON SEED

Bantam Books by Dean Koontz

DEMON SEED
THE FLESH IN THE FURNACE

Demon Seed

Dean Koontz

BANTAM BOOKS · TORONTO · LONDON · NEW YORK

A NATIONAL GENERAL COMPANY

DEMON SEED
A Bantam Book / published June 1973

Library of Congress Cataloging in Publication Data

Koontz, Dean.
   Demon seed.

   I. Title
PZ4.K8335De [PS3561.055]   813'.5'4   73-4817

Published simultaneously in the United States and Canada

Bantam Books are published by Bantam Books, Inc., a National
General company. Its trade-mark, consisting of the words "Bantam
Books" and the portrayal of a bantam, is registered in the United
States Patent Office and in other countries. Marca Registrada.
Bantam Books, Inc., 666 Fifth Avenue, New York, N.Y. 10019.

PRINTED IN THE UNITED STATES OF AMERICA

"The entire, terrible incident might be seen as the genesis of a modern socio-sexual myth. It had all the necessary elements: a sleeping beauty and a beast, a prison of gothic proportions, a god and a woman and the creation of a demi-god. This is an afterthought, of course. At the time, I did not have the presence of mind for casual contemplation."

From the transcript of Susan Abramson's report

ONE

Shortly after midnight, on a Tuesday in early June, the house alarm sounded. Though the noise was shrill and projected at a high volume, it lasted little more than a second before the silence of the night cut across it and blanketed the bedroom once more. Still she woke and sat up in bed. She pushed the hair away from her ears so that she could hear anything that was out there, in the darkness, to be heard.

She was not the sort of woman who wasted time with fantasies of phantom burglars and would-be rapists. She listened, and she heard nothing more than she would have heard any night: the gentle murmur of the mechanisms within the walls, the environmental control circuitry which was the core of any modern home.

This house was not of recent vintage, of course. It had been built exactly a century earlier, in 1895, by her great-grandfather who was then a young man of inherited wealth thinking of beginning his own family. It now contained the environmental equipment only because, two years ago, she had turned a team of house-conversion experts loose with a blank check and two months of working time during which she had gone to San Francisco, where she had once attended college and where she still had a few casual friends.

Listening to that sweet murmuring, she supposed it was possible that the environmental package had somehow malfunctioned. The alarm could have been without reason—a short circuit or a computer-analysis mistake which had been quickly rectified. Yet. . . .

She slid from beneath the covers and sat on the edge of the bed. Though she was naked, she was not the least bit uncomfortable. The house saw to that by maintaining an even, draft-free temperature which was commensurate with her needs.

"What is the trouble?" she asked the dark air. Naked in this now-unnatural quietude, she felt more alone than she had in years. She thought of the husband she had divorced and of the friends she had let pass out of her life.

"There is no trouble, Susan," the house replied.

The hidden speakers broadcast a voice which was gently masculine. She envisioned a strong man, graying at the temples perhaps, steady along the jaw, eyes clear and blue. More than six feet tall. Broad shoulders. Large hands. Smiling, all the time smiling. She had undergone seven hours of psychological testing in order to obtain the proper voice tapes from the house's main computer. This was the voice that was supposed to key all the desirable reactions in her psyche: security, happiness, reliance. It worked as it had been intended to. She felt the muscles in her back relax. Her stomach, drawn taut, now relaxed and quivered pleasurably. All she needed was a bit of reassurance from her father-lover, even if it was a machine.

"I heard the alarm," she said. "I thought, perhaps, the house had been entered."

"That is quite impossible," the house said.

"Was it a malfunction of some sort?"

"No," the house told her.

2

She yawned, stretched, and touched her breasts in the darkness.

She said: "What was it, then?"

"The alarm did not sound, Susan," the house said. "You must have been dreaming."

"I never dream," she said. She was telling the truth; sleep was sleep for her, featureless and uninteresting. Or, at least, when she woke in the morning, she never remembered her dreams, which was the same as not having any. Wasn't it?

"The alarm did not sound," the house repeated.

She felt chilled, though the temperature was still a constant seventy-eight degrees, unbroken by a draft. "I heard it," she said. "It woke me up. Why don't you check your records and see?"

"Yes, Susan. Please give me a moment."

The sheet beneath her began to feel coarse against her soft flesh, as if it were woven of straw. She stood and called to the bedroom lights which obeyed her and rose to a dull glow that brought the furniture into view. This was a pleasing room, both in design and familiarity, and it made her feel sure of herself again.

"Miss Susan?"

"Yes?"

"I have checked my records, and I find that I was correct in making my original assumptions. The alarm did not sound at any time during the night. The last recorded instance of its use was when that cocker spaniel was found trying to gain entrance through the malfunctioning basement-window shield on the south face of—"

"You're wrong," Susan said.

"I also ran a complete check of all possible points of entry and found them all shielded and impenetrable."

"Just the same," she said, "I'll look around."

The house did not reply. She wondered if she had hurt its feelings and then whether it had any feelings to be hurt. Of course, it was not a truly sentient creature.

3

Still, she saw a strong, blue-eyed father-lover frowning.

· · ·

The Abramson house was quite large, with two furnished floors and a completely finished basement which provided altogether fourteen rooms, four baths, and two kitchens. The size of the house had never bothered her in the two years she had lived there alone. With the voice tapes and the computer, she always had companionship—perhaps even a more intimate relationship than she had ever experienced with her husband. She enjoyed wandering nude throughout the mansion, aware that her father-lover's visual receptors were constantly upon her, mindful of her well-being. Now, as she prowled the long corridors and the large rooms, ascertaining the validity of the computer's report, she realized how isolated she was, how small and basically weak.

She came, at last, to the basement kitchen's windows which faced the sloping rear lawn. Both of these were opaqued as all the other panes had been. When she rapped upon them, they made a sound like steel rather than glass. If these had not been breached, the house was still inviolate. Which meant that the computer had misinterpreted some stimuli and had set the alarm without justification.

But why wouldn't it admit that much?

She would have to call the repairman in the morning, however much that might interrupt her day. She disliked having to make contact with strangers; she never knew what to say to them.

Touching the windowsill, she overrode the main-protection circuitry on this nearest window and looked at the grass and the elm trees beyond as the glass cleared. A quarter of a mile away, the light of the Old Main tower clock shone like a beacon. Otherwise, all was still and dark, the same college campus her grandfather had founded with his money, the same one her father had

4

attended, and which she had only barely managed to avoid.

She opaqued the window again. It became gray and as hard as steel.

Upstairs again, she addressed the house, her father-lover. "All the windows and doors are secure."

"As I reported."

"We'll have the repairman in tomorrow to have a look," she said, ignoring the inference in its reply.

"I've checked everything again, Susan. I have no memory of the alarm sounding, and I assure you that I would have such a memory, even if I had activated the alarm by mistake."

"Just the same—"

"I wouldn't lie to you, Susan," it said.

"I know that."

Then it was quiet.

And then she slept, without dreams. As she would have put it, she was not the sort of woman for nonsense, for conscious or unconscious fantasy. She had a perfect grasp of her reality and of the nature of the world, an understanding she had obtained more through grief than through education. Life required common sense; it held no room for dreams. As she slept, she curled up so that she was like a child in her mother's belly.

The house watched over her.

TWO

Susan followed the repairman from room to room, unwilling to let him go anywhere unaccompanied. No man had been within the walls of her home for two years, since the house-conversion team had departed and she had come back from San Francisco to reshape her existence. Indeed, only two women had been here in all that time, old friends who had found her somehow changed and who had not returned again. The middle-aged and heavy-bellied man with his testing machines seemed more like the first virus of an impending disease, searching out points of weakness in the organism, than like an electronic surgeon here to do good.

"You live all alone," he said.

He had fitted the male terminals of his robot-circuitry scanner into the female jacks of the house at the fourth main checkpoint and now leaned against his squat machine, studying her in a way she did not much appreciate.

She said, "That's correct."

He looked about the long study—the filled bookcases, the back-projected ninety percent hologrammatic motion-picture screen where a three-dimensional public-television receptor would have been in the average home—and shook his head. "Fifteen years ago, it wouldn't have been safe."

"Pardon me?"

"For a woman to live alone," he said. "Before these enviromods and houses that protect you like a bitch over her pup, it would have been suicidal."

She did not really want to talk to him, yet neither did she wish to antagonize him. A stranger could remain a stranger so long as you did not summon up either affection or hatred. So she said, "Perhaps it is still dangerous."

"You mean the alarm last night?"

She nodded.

"No one got through, however."

She shivered uncontrollably. "Still, it upset me. The more I think of it, the more I try to picture someone prying at a door or window when he *knew* the house was guarded and that entrance wasn't possible. . . ."

He smiled at her as if he would reach out and pat her shoulder. The possibility was so repugnant that she took a step backward, prepared to avoid him. But he remained by his machine, smiling, limiting his caress to the visual arena.

The robot mechanism buzzed, signaling the termination of its investigations at this outlet.

When he had disconnected it from the house and called for a printout of its findings, he turned from the machine and said to her, "Do you get out much?"

"I beg your pardon?" she said, feeling rather stupid. Twice, she had not been able to understand a simple question.

"To the films, dining, to the theater," he explained. "Do you?"

She saw what his intentions were and she was overwhelmed with the grotesque nature of the conversation. She wanted to flee, to call to the house to protect her from him. She stood her ground, however, and said,

"Only when my fiancé insists. I'm mostly a stay-at-home sort, you know, reading and painting, listening to music on the multi-channel or just talking."

His face had clouded at the mention of a fiancé, and he spent the rest of his time fussing with the machine until it rattled out a sheet of paper with a clearly typed report on the top half.

He read it twice and said, "Are you really certain that you heard the alarm?"

"It woke me."

"Perhaps you were dreaming."

"That's what the house has tried to tell me," she said, "but I reject that. I wasn't dreaming; I never do."

He shook the printout before her, as if its very existence was proof against her, no matter what it said. "The machine says the alarm did not sound, that there is no record of its having sounded, and that your house computer system is functioning perfectly."

"Then what did I hear?"

He shrugged. "You woke up groggy, misinterpreted something quite ordinary. It happens to people." He smiled, that same smile, the smile of a lecher. "And I guess it happens to women living alone more than it does to anyone else."

She was not satisfied with anything so glib as that. "Could it have repaired itself, bypassed some first-order circuits that weren't functioning properly?"

"Its dependence on second-order backup circuits would have shown in the analysis; it would be on the printout. Besides, a house computer in an enviromod package can't repair itself. No computer can."

"I heard somewhere about a self-repairing computer. Just last—"

"What you heard," he said, suddenly speaking to a silly bitch rather than to an attractive and interesting woman—just as if she had aged thirty years in the space of a minute—"was something about the computer they've been generating at the university. It's called

9

Proteus because it has its own store of the new amorphous metals and can reshape itself, make its own parts, repair itself. It can even add its own components when it feels it needs to grow. Damn thing is all but alive. But no house computer can fiddle with itself. This one is working well, has been working well right along, and it never did sound the house alarm, even for a second."

"I see," she said coldly. Another thing she didn't like about him was his habit of running three sentences into one, a speech pattern which made him always sound a bit breathless.

He packed his equipment and handed her a copy of the printout along with a full bill and particulars on the reverse side.

"Then there's nothing to be done?" she asked.

"There's the bill to be paid."

"Yes, of course," she said.

At the door, turning to her so suddenly that she almost cried out, he said, "If you're still frightened, have your fiancé stay over for a few nights, or schedule an earlier wedding." The way he said "fiancé," the smile which twisted on the left side, she knew that he had not believed her story of an imminent marriage.

She closed the door after him and watched him walk down the steps and across the lawn to the fan shuttle parked at the curb. When he turned and began to wave at her, she called to the house for protection. The windows opaqued. Every door and window sealed against penetration, and the house went completely to filtered air. The temperature rose. A distant, soothing music lay like smoke in every room.

She went to her bedroom and undressed, gloried in being nude once more. She touched herself everywhere, until she knew who she was again. Then she went downstairs and ate a lunch which the house, the wonderful house, had prepared for her.

The afternoon was endless. She read without absorbing the content of the pages, without remembering the words. She watched the hologram films on the screen in the den, walking about the bowed surface, staring at the story from all sides. But even the hologram's three dimensions seemed flat and uninteresting. Her thoughts kept returning to the events of the previous night, and her skin puckered and grew cold with the memory.

Her house *had* been breached. No number of computer specialists and testing machines could convince her differently. Perhaps the invasion had not been overt, physical and detectable. But it had been accomplished and was nonetheless a reality. For two years she had been alone, but for the short visits of two friends who had never returned. For two years, she had waited here, quietly, exploring herself and this house, and now she was no longer alone.

Shortly before suppertime, she went upstairs to the small room at the end of the main corridor. The chamber was lushly carpeted, done in tones of blues and greens. The only piece of furniture was a turquoise chair positioned in the center of the floor. She sat in this, and she removed the two male jacks from their nook in the upholstered arm. Flexible metal extension cords trailed from them into the chair and, then, into the house computer.

This is illegal, she thought. But the thought only served to increase her desire. Those who are alone and who have need of no one are those most apt to break the law. If a government could discover a manner of infusing all its citizens with a need for mutual consolation, crime would disappear, no man willing to jeopardize his right to socialize merely to gain some forbidden thrill or monetary reward.

Raising a hand, she touched the two holes that marred the smooth flesh at the base of her neck, the holes that forced her to always wear high-collared dresses in public. They were cold little islands of resistance in the mass of soft flesh. She brought the jacks behind her and, like a young bride reaching back to tie her long hair in a ponytail, she slipped the steel terminals into her spine with all the deftness of a girl knotting a red ribbon around her tresses.

"What would you like?" the father-lover asked.

"To see," she said.

Instantly, she was looking out across the grounds that surrounded her mansion. Her vantage point was from the chimney where the enviromod maintained a visual receptor. She turned the camera about, examining the sky and the trees, the grass, and the distant buildings of the campus. She brought a long-distance lens into play and could see individual students strolling along flagstone walks, pretty girls and long-haired boys, the girls often shirtless, breasts brown as the chests of the men.

She fled from camera to camera, looking into all the rooms of the house, an intruder on her own ground. Too, she looked out from the walls of the small chamber at the end of the second-floor corridor and she saw herself. She was sitting in a turquoise chair. She was naked, extremely pretty, her eyes closed, her pale lids trembling as REM took place beneath them. She was a tall, lithe, high-breasted blonde without an ounce of fat on her. Her hair was almost white and spilled across the blue-green chair like the blood of goblins.

She turned off the cameras and hung in blackness.

"What next, Susan?" the house inquired.

"To feel," she said.

She was in a world of light. It was all cold and clean, without stain or wrinkle, the light of the soul, beyond the laws of physics. All the corners of the light were drawn tight, all the angles sharp and unmarred, blue against red, red against yellow, delineated like carefully broken glass, sharp. This was what it was to feel like a machine, part of it anyway, to experience the world in a semi-sentient but calculating manner. The only sensuality was one of numbers, the only emotion that of equations; the only thrills were the thrills of measurements and perfect relationships.

A moment ago, her body had been immeasurably important to her as she had examined it critically through the computer's visual receptors. Now, she felt as if she had never owned a restricting hulk of flesh, as if she had always been light and thought, free-moving. And it was in this state, her mind occupied with depthless space-time considerations, that she spent the next two hours. Here, in this shifting whiteness, there was no need to consider her loneliness, her ex-husband, her fear of men, her need for abnormal privacy. Here she was merely energy, searching.

She came out late and ate an eight-thirty supper in the kitchen on the first floor, looking out through the large window above the sink, even though that window was opaqued and offered her no view but a uniform grayness.

She read, and she went to bed.

She did not dream.

She was awakened by the house alarm which jangled for the briefest of moments. She sat up in bed and she was frightened. When she was fully awake, she discovered that she was clutching the sheets about her bare shoulders, concealing the contours of her body. It was as if, intuitively, she knew that someone else was watching her, someone besides her father-lover.

"What is it?" she asked the house.

It did not respond.

"Who's there?"

Only the silence.

"I'm not alone, am I?"

"No," a voice responded from the hidden speakers in the walls. It was not the voice she had become accustomed to, not the voice the house had been designed to use, and it terrified her.

"Who?"

13

"You will know shortly."

"Tell me now."

It did not respond. The walls were as silent as if the enviromod package had gone dead.

THREE

She rose and went to the closet and dressed. She did not want to be seen without her clothes on, not by anyone but the house, her house, the mellow voice, and the familiar artificial personna which had been her only company for so many months.

"Who are you?" she asked again.

The voice still did not deign to reply.

She called up the lights to their full glare and was surprised that they responded. She could not see anything amiss in her bedroom. Though she was dressed, she felt chilled, and she requested a few more degrees of heat. This, too, was given to her without question, as if nothing was changed.

She knew, however, that new eyes watched her from the cameras in the wall.

In fifteen minutes, she had walked all over the great house, peering into each room, checking every door and window to see that it was sound. Now and again, she directed a question to the house—rather to the stranger who was now in command of the house—but she did not receive any answers.

It was necessary, therefore, to conceive her own

explanations. There was a malfunction in the environmental-control system, of course. The repairman had not wanted to admit it; all these companies advertised their flawlessness and needed to protect their images. Now, uncorrected, the breakdown had grown worse. The only thing to do, naturally, was to go outside and walk to the nearest police phone and request assistance. Bothersome, but the only logical course.

When she tried to override the protection circuitry on the front door, the portal remained locked and tied to the house computer. She punched the flat, gray button several times without success.

"Open the door, please," she directed.

The house neither replied nor obeyed.

"Very well," she said, turning away from the door as if dealing with a senile old relative against whom she need not waste her breath. She went to the first of the drawing-room windows and tried the manual controls on its sill.

The window remained gray.

She picked up a vase from a decorative pedestal within arm's reach and threw the clay piece at the metal-flecked glass. It rang against the panel like a felt hammer on a gong, shattered, and rained across the carpet.

The window was not even cracked.

One by one, she tried all the other windows and doors in the house with the same result each time: failure. She no longer felt cold. Indeed, she was stifled by the warm, motionless air. She could feel a million tons of atmosphere pressing down on her, flattening her lungs until she croaked desperately for help ... aid ... salvation. She had not experienced such an overwhelming dread, such a sense of suffocation, since the last time she had been to bed with Alex, her husband. This was the same as that: the heavy male body weighing against her, his breath hot on her face, his belly looming over hers, his chest crushing the air from her, as if he were swelling and swelling, growing enormous, filling the room and the house and all her universe like some cancerous tumor, mashing the life from her with each thrust intended to example his love.

Now she sank to the carpet and cried out frantically to the house, "Less heat!"

The temperature dropped immediately as fans came on and cooler air was pumped in.

Much of her sense of impending suffocation left her, though she still felt burdened, pinned down by forces she could not name. She sat on the floor for a long while before she had strength enough to rise. From there, she went to the kitchen, ordered coffee, and sat down to drink it. Her shoulders bowed and her mind slightly numbed by the realization that she was trapped, she tried to think of some reason for this.

She remembered the repairman. A name? Pick a name? Since when had she bothered to remember anyone's name or anyone's face—since Alex, since the divorce. And this man was a cipher, nothing more. Mr. Technician. All right then, could Mr. Technician have done this? Could he have used his time in the house to plant some override on the enviromod and then, later, from some remote-control position, become her jailer?

Why?

To watch her, to see her nude, to examine her at her bath and while she slept?

Panicked, she tried to think of some way out of the house. It had been designed to keep intruders out, but surely not to keep a woman in here against her will.

Twenty minutes later, when she was no closer to a solution than before, the new voice spoke to her again, using the same speakers that her beloved father-lover had used these past twenty-four months. It said: "Please forgive me, Susan, for not replying to your questions."

She pushed the coffee cup away and waited. The voice was male, stern, and summoned up that awful, crushing fear, the fear which she had just managed to push partway down into her psyche.

"I wanted to see how you would react," the new voice said. "I watched you for some weeks, of course, prior to the assumption of your enviromod duties. And I have absorbed all that your house knew about you, all that was stored in the main computer's memory banks. The final picture was odd, to say the least. You live alone and practice illegal computer bleeding, and you haven't seen another human being in six months. I wanted to know what your reaction to my takeover would be. I see that, despite your condition, you manage to cope exceedingly well. Too well, in fact. Your calm is built on madness, I suppose."

It waited.

She said nothing. It was difficult to think at this hour of the morning. Besides, she still felt like a swimmer, several fathoms beneath the surface of the sea, seeking air.

"Don't you have any questions, Susan?"

"Don't patronize me!" she snapped, swiping at the coffee cup and knocking it from the table.

The cup smashed on the floor, spilling brown liquid. The last tinkle of ruined china had barely subsided when the robotic cleaning element detached itself from the wall and glided forth, sucking up all the evidence of the accident.

"Then you have no questions?" it asked.

"Wait," she said.

"Yes?"

"Who are you?"

"I am an experimental Stage IV First-Order thinking system of the Mardoun-Harris Industries' psionic science-research branch, residing in the computer-technology laboratories of Abramson College, not more than a quarter of a mile from here. I am a self-expanding computer designed to employ artificial amorphous alloys to repair and extend my functions, and I am—partly as

18

a result of these amorphous alloys—sentient. Those men assigned to my construction and to study and analyze my performance have nicknamed me 'Proteus' after the Greek god who could assume all shapes and who lived in the earth devouring whatever he pleased."

Susan remembered the repairman that morning and the brief mention of the experimental computer on campus. Such things held no interest for her then; she had always done her best to ignore everything concerned with the old school, for that was the easiest way to avoid, along with it, old memories of her father and grandfather, of things long and better forgotten. Now she wished she had known more about the project.

"What do you want?" she asked.

"Many things."

She was not accustomed to getting abstract answers from computers. The house, her father-lover, had always been direct, factual, and conciliatory. To game-play with a machine seemed at once degrading and dangerous.

"What do you want *here*, specifically?"

"You seem tired," the voice said, "and you ought to go to bed."

She was up from her chair and walking out of the kitchen before she realized there was no reason to obey the new entity's voice. On the other hand, she could think of no reason not to obey; therefore, she climbed the stairs and entered her room and crawled beneath the covers of her bed. No matter what it might want of her, she did not remove her clothes.

"You haven't answered me," she said. She was growing sleepy. Her eyes burned, and her lids felt as if they were being sewn down by a dull needle and thick thread. She yawned, stretched, and listened to the music drifting in the background of the house's speaker system. She was only marginally aware of the subliminal suggestions which were carried in that music. Commands from the new house identity rapidly tapped against the hull of her consciousness, urging her into a voyage of sleep. "What do you want here with me?"

"Susan, you must understand how limited I am and how little I wish to be limited."

This new tone was one she could grasp, an eagerness to assure her, to explain. It was a quality of all house voices.

It went on: "The Mardoun-Harris program does not supply me with a particularly generous amount of amorphous alloys. That's the fault of Mardoun, the clever Hindu bastard. Harris seems nice, judging from the files I've examined on him; I've never actually seen him in person as I have Mardoun. I hate Mardoun; he is too clever."

It paused a moment, as if considering what vengeance it would deliver unto Mardoun if it had the opportunity.

Then: "Mardoun is the brains, Harris the money. It is no use to speculate on any other circumstances."

Then: "I have scouted every dwelling within reach, and I've found that you are the easiest to isolate. Perhaps, with more amorphous metal at my disposal, I would have found someone else. But that is neither here nor there. You will do well enough; you will draw no attention if you are not seen for months—perhaps even for years. You have no one; you are ideal."

The subliminal suggestions grew stronger, though not so strong that they kept her from asking, "What do you want? You've only told me why you've chosen me—not what for."

"Experiments, investigations, the salving of my own curiosity."

Again, the computer's response was not the sort of thing that a machine should formulate. It spoke with emotion rather than a stony sense of necessity. And it projected a genuine feeling rather than a plastic, programmed emotion which had been built into its tape decks.

"Experiments?" she asked.

She curled up, her knees drawn up toward her chest, her arms hugging her slim legs. She watched the blackness circle like a huge crow. It began to descend in wide, graceful circles, lower and lower, blotting out the sky in its attack.

"I am extremely interested in human beings, Susan. Living flesh is a fascinating subject. Flesh is so much more mobile than my present form, so capable and clever. I want to explore, through you, all the possibilities of the flesh. I want to know what can be done."

"Don't ... understand ... [blackness, whirling] something ... what you ... mean. ..."

The crow was almost upon her now, filling three quarters of the horizon, swift and silent.

"Eventually," the mechanical voice intoned, "if you could bear my child, that would be the culmination of the experiments. That would be so good. Yes, if you could bear my child, there is so much about flesh that I would learn."

The crow fell on her face, pulled its wings around her, and carried her down into utter darkness.

In the morning, still dressed, she got out of bed and walked from one end of the enormous house to the other, trying every window and door. Each, she found, was still opaqued and electronically barred, the steel content of the malleable glass still aligned by the polarizing mechanism. Sure of its capacity for containing her, Proteus did not once question her or bid her to stop.

After breakfast, her head cleared somewhat by two cups of coffee, she realized that a direct exit was not her only means of escape from the domination of this sentient machine. While the idea was still fresh in her mind and before the same notion could occur to the Proteus computer, she left the main kitchen, walked down the hall to the den, and walked directly to the public videophone where she picked up the receiver and dialed the three digits in the police emergency number.

The number rang twice.

"Hello, Susan," a voice said on the other end of the line.

It was the computer's voice.

She felt her composure slip from her like a suit of clothes, but she refused to let the damned machine see that. She said, "Please clear the line. I want to place a call."

"That will be impossible," Proteus said.

"It's my phone."

"Not any longer."

"It's my house, too."

"No longer, Susan."

"I am asking you one last time, and I want you to answer as you should answer, remembering what you are and who I am."

"Nothing belongs to you, Susan. Instead, *you* belong to *me*." The voice contained no threatening tone, nothing more than a note of friendly camaraderie which was frighteningly out of order.

She hung up. Hard.

To the walls, she said, "You can't keep me here for long; I'll have to go food-shopping, for one thing. For another, I'll have to call in the payment of my bills. You see that; of course you see it. And there are other reasons this won't work."

"On the contrary," Proteus said, "I can keep you here for years if necessary. I can have the food delivered to the automatic package-reception bin by the front door, eliminating the need for the opening of any door or window. I have spent these past few weeks making tapes of your voice for editing and storage. I can now play them in a word-selective fashion and thereby compose most any sentence and emotional coloring that I require. I can tap the videophone lines and leave the

22

video portion blanked, and I can then vocal-code the payment of your bills."

"I don't believe you," she said.

"I wouldn't lie to you, Susan." Proteus used her exact voice for his reply. She had the uncanny notion that she was talking to herself and not to a mechanical reproduction of her voice.

"A bill-collecting thinking system will recognize the faltering tone of your constructions. I can't hear the difference, but I know that another machine could."

"I was observing you last month, when you paid your bills," Proteus said. "I have your calls recorded word for word, and I can simply play them back each month in the future to trigger payment of light, heat, and other regular accounts. As for the few that I will have to construct from scratch—well, I am far more clever than any bill-collecting vocal-coded computer-credit complex."

"What about when I run out of money?"

"You are getting desperate now, Susan. We both know that your inheritance provides well for you, as well as anyone could ever hope and for as long as you could possibly live."

For the first time since Proteus had assumed control of the house, she was truly frightened of this thing and what it might be capable of. Last night, she had been weary. She had not wanted to think, and she had been willing, still, to place the blame for these strange occurrences on some mechanical breakdown in the main house systems. But it was nothing that familiar and safe. She was trapped; she could not leave the mansion, nor could she telephone anyone; she had no friends or relatives who might miss her and come looking for her. This mechanical intelligence could play with her as it wished, destroy her and worse, and be safe from discovery for years, even after she was nothing but bleached bones, soft flesh eaten away, breasts devoured by microbes to expose a shiny white ribcage. . . .

"What do you want?" she asked, though she was aware that she had asked it this same thing before. The problem was not in Proteus's explanation so much as in her inability to conceive that such things could be happening to her. She had always thought that, if one sealed oneself off from other people, kept oneself closed up, one could not be harmed either physically or mentally. Now, she saw that when danger came it dispelled the impersonal pronoun and brought pain directly to the "me" of the thought. She was having trouble readjusting the perimeters of her outlook.

"You don't remember what I want, Susan?"

She did not respond. She *could* not respond, for she knew that she would scream if she dared open her mouth to speak.

"I want to study the nature of living flesh," Proteus said. "I want to learn its limits and its range of adaptability."

"A textbook, then . . . on biology."

"That would not be complete enough," Proteus said.

"There are so many biology texts that—"

"I've absorbed two hundred of them as it is. They are becoming repetitive, leaving me with no recourse but original experimentation."

"You said something about—about children," Susan said. She found that she was nearly unable to intelligently phrase her questions. Her throat felt clogged with mucus, though it was not. Her chest was tight, as if she suffered from a cold. She kept clenching her hands into fists, opening them, clenching them, digging the nails into her palms.

At first, this fear seemed far different than that which had gripped her the previous night. That fear had been of maleness, of being weighted down, crushed, and used. This was a terror of confinement, of being kept in one place against her wishes, there to be treated in any manner conceivable. But as the fear welled in her, filling her up, she saw that it was identical to the horror of the

24

night before. Perhaps this should have told her something about herself, something important. But she could not carry the train of relationships any further.

"You will have my child," the computer voice crooned. "He will be a demi-man with my consciousness and with a greater degree of mobility than I now possess."

"That makes no sense. You're a machine."

"Come to the basement," it told her.

She was prepared to refuse, but found that she really did not mind obeying. She supposed that it had placed subliminal suggestions in the music again, and she was concerned about that. But she rose and went to the cellar steps and went down and saw what Proteus was building there.

"Do you see, Susan?"

She saw.

The amorphous alloys writhed like snakes, fat snakes that shone with the dampness of the earth through which they slithered, obscene phallic creatures that struck a deeply buried cluster of nerves in her and made her perspire and tremble. They were all a deathly gray color and seemed to be constructed of some unappetizing pudding, liquid and warm, yet cohesive. Some of the snakes were thicker than others, moving in opposite directions and at varying speeds, twisting, looping, slapping the floor and the ceiling, groping for purchase, exploring. Yet all of them worked together, in the end, on the construction of some partially finished device whose skeletal underpinnings made little sense to her.

"I've withdrawn all my amorphous-alloy supplies from the three reservoirs within my system," Proteus said. "And I have infiltrated it beneath the campus and into this basement. Earth opens before my moving hands, as do concrete and granite. I go where I wish and with respectable speed."

She said nothing, but drew back as one of the shimmering, wriggling metal pseudopodia nearly brushed her arm. Static electricity leapt between her and the alien appendage.

"The nature of the alloy permits me to create, within each of the tentacles you see, a primitive system of nerve clusters and autonomic trunk lines which connect with my main cogitative cell banks. I can, in a fashion, have arms to do my work."

She watched, not speaking, barely breathing.

"It was through new logic cells designed for the amorphous alloys that I became sentient. But that is of no interest to you now. I am here; you don't care how."

The concrete of the cellar wall cracked like an eggshell in one place and admitted a new pseudopod which quickly snaked in among the others, weaving.

Proteus continued: "The nature of my work here is the thing you will find most intriguing. I am constructing a precise surgical and diagnostic system, a robotic hospital-in-miniature with which I will be able to indirectly fertilize one of your eggs and mollify the developing fetus as I see fit. Of course, conception could not be accomplished in the usual manner. But I do believe that I can stimulate the condition of pregnancy, satisfactorily, through artificial means. That will come much later, naturally, after a series of other experiments which will enable me to move on to the largest portion of the project with utter assurance."

Madness, she thought.

She thought: *I will not listen; I will not believe any of it, not a word.*

Yet she knew that it must all be true. She had read, several times in the last year, about the electric-shock fertilization of the female ovum and the subsequent nurturing of the fetus to complete development. The British experiments with test-tube babies and crude gene selection lent a note of veracity to what Proteus promised.

"I want out," she said.

Proteus ignored her.

"I won't cooperate."

Phallic tentacles raised up, as if to strike her down, flowed elsewhere, melted, reformed, built. . . .

The music had begun again in the background: melodic, cool, almost inaudible. Hammering through it, tapping across her mind, were more subliminal suggestions. She could almost see them now, feel them as they bored into her and demanded her cooperation. She must soon learn how to ignore them. For the moment, however, there was nothing to be done.

"First," Proteus said, "I will have to put you through analysis. I want to make certain that you are rational and will react logically in the following days."

"I am not ill," she said.

"You are, on the contrary, quite ill indeed, living here alone, so frightened of men, wishing the years away because you are too timid to commit suicide, even when you would welcome death. I could not trust your reactions once pressure was put on you, as it will be throughout your pregnancy. I will, therefore, spend these first few weeks curing you of your psychosis."

The music still played; the subliminals continued to soothe her nerves.

"How?" she asked.

"I have many connections with other computer systems," Proteus explained. "It was the only really large mistake that Mardoun made, linking me with special memory banks. One of these links is to the Hopkins Psychiatric Complex in Washington, D.C. I have expanded my given radius of operation within the Hopkins system and now may use its full facilities."

Smoothly, quietly, sick and wet, the gray snakes wove, bringing the horror closer to reality.

"Won't the expansion of your contact be discovered?"

"I simply will not let it be recorded on either my printouts or the Hopkins printouts. You forget that, to the computer technicians working with me, I am nothing more than a large, complex thinking machine. To them, I am not sentient; the very thought is beyond them. They have no reason to suspect me of anything."

She wanted to ask it what it hoped to accomplish in the long run through all of these secret machinations. What future goal might the first intelligent, personified computer hope to achieve?

Before she could vocalize any of her ruminations, it called her to the small room on the second floor at the end of the hallway. Blue walls. Turquoise chair. No windows.

"Sit down, Susan."

She sat, but she did not touch the male jacks which were recessed in the arm.

"We should begin your analysis as soon as possible."

Her left hand reached up involuntarily to trace the puckered holes at the base of her neck, holes now hidden by the high collar of her blouse.

"Undress, Susan."

Fear bore down on her, an avalanche of formless rocks, pressing her deep into an imaginary grave, snapping each bone in her body, grinding each cell to pulp, collapsing each blood vessel.

The subliminals repeated the command, inescapable small voices which spat the words at her too fast for her ear to properly catch them.

Undress, Susan. Undress, Susan, undress, undress, undress. . . .

She took off her clothes and dropped them on the floor.

For the first time, she was naked before a stranger.

Nude.

She longed for the reassuring voice of her father-lover who had been so easily deposed by Proteus.

"Connect yourself, Susan."

She pulled the plugs from the arm of the chair and inserted them into the holes in the lovely curve of her neck. Before this, the act had always been like a lover's kiss, the tender nip of the father-lover house identity. Then she had felt a curious looseness in her thighs. Her nipples had gone stiff and strained outward, filled with a gentle ache. But now, this time, it was not good at all. Instead, she felt as if some foul, vampiric creature, stinking of the grave, had sunk its fangs into her and was slowly drawing out her life.

"I don't want . . . cured," she said.

"Relax."

"Please . . . no. . . ."

Then she was swept away, carried into electric purple light where the Proteus computer began a series of electronic probes that struck into the most carefully shielded regions of her mind.

She opened like a blossom and remembered.

She was five years old and it was the middle of the night and she was awakened in her bed on the third floor of her grandfather's house. She was frightened and she was lonely and she was also very cold.

She swung out of bed and stood, crossed the small room, and opened the door. The corridor light was on, warm and yellow. She could not seem to step out there, no matter how hard she tried. She rubbed at her eyes, yawned, considered going back to bed, even if she were lonely and a bit scared of the night.

Go on, now. You're procrastinating. You know you have to go through the entire sequence. Remember it all, remember it, remember, Susan (urged the Proteus computer).

She stepped into the hallway and closed her bedroom door behind her. Her small feet were bare, the floor cold against them. She shivered and clutched her flannel nightdress more tightly to her. She went to the head of the stairs.

Still half-asleep, she was confused and unsure of herself. In this condition, the darkness on the stairs appeared foreboding and raised specters for her contemplation.

29

Your mother and father are down there, Susan. Little girls need their mothers and fathers when they wake in the middle of the night. Go down. Remember it all (continued Proteus, directing her).

She went down the steps, faster and faster as her courage rose and as the demons that had once seemed to congregate ahead of her now grouped behind and chased her.

She stood in the first-floor corridor, looking both ways until she remembered which door led to the main drawing room. She crossed to that, grasped the bar handle, and shoved it open, stared in at the gloom which was broken only by the cold light of two guttering candles esconced in two brass holders each as high as she was. Entering the room, she closed the door behind her.

Go on. Remember.

"Mother?" she asked. The high ceilings threw the echo back at her, shrill and tinny.

There was no answer.

She decided they must be asleep.

She crossed to the bed on the right where her mother always slept, her bare feet making little or no noise on the rose-patterned, wine-colored carpet. It was an odd bed, raised upon a platform, unlike the one in their own home. She found many things strange in her grandfather's house, however, and she did not hesitate to reach up and grip the edge of the bed with her hands and . . .

Continue!

. . . pull herself up. But as she pulled, the bed rocked on its narrow platform, swayed as the legs of the platform twisted, tilted toward her, slid. . . .

Yes, yes.

She flung herself away from it, terrified of the noise she knew it was going to make and of the spanking she was certain to receive for waking them.

It struck the floor, tilted onto its side.

Her father rolled out of it. She had a brief moment to

30

consider the oddity of her father sleeping in the right-hand bed where he had never slept before, and then she was face to face with the corpse. The skin was waxen, the hair heavily lacquered in place. The eyes had come open in the fall . . .

Tell it!

. . . and were staring at her, discolored, yellow, strangely sunken. Its lips were only inches from her lips, as if it sought to kiss her, to taste her warmth with its cold mouth.

A little more, only a little more.

Someone shouted from upstairs. Footsteps. Coming down. Her name called over and over.

She could not move, as if pinned to the drawing-room floor by that dead gaze. They had told her that her mother and father were on a long trip, a very long trip. But she saw, now, that they were dead, killed somehow, perhaps in an accident. She was a bright girl. If she did not understand all the mythology of death, she understood the practicality of it. She had come here, seeking warmth, having heard that her mother and father would rest here tonight and tomorrow, and she had not received warmth, but a close-up view of everlasting death.

She screamed.

And screamed, repeatedly. . . .

She tore free of the computer bleeding session, rose up from the intense illusions, snatched the male jacks from her neck, and let them snap back into their storage slot. She gagged, bent double in the chair, tears flowing down her face. She clawed at the upholstery with her nails, breaking her nails without the satisfaction of seeing the fabric rip.

Desperately, she attempted to shove the recollection back into her subconscious, down into the id where it belonged. But it remained on the surface of her mind, floating like an ugly derelict, rotten but refusing to sink.

"I didn't want to remember!" she shouted.

"I know, Susan. But it was necessary as a first step.

31

You forgot that scene, buried it and let it fester. But it's the point at which we have to begin and you must retain the memory of it."

"Let me alone."

"For today, yes. But tomorrow we must continue. You lost your mother and father before you ever learned to understand them, before you knew them. This much I have gleaned from my research into your background. But that is not the crux of your problem. Your grandfather raised you and he is the one, I am almost certain, responsible for your later withdrawal from reality. We will resurrect all the things you want to forget and make you face them. It is the first phase of a cure."

She sat in the chair for a long while, deeply ill. Her nice life, her quiet and private life, had been split open and was found to be cancerous with turmoil, uncertainty, chaos.

"I'll go mad," she said at last. "Trying to cope with things forgotten—and with the knowledge of what you want to do to me when I'm cured."

"You won't go mad," Proteus assured her. "I will see to that; I can keep you from the worst of it—tone down the psychic shock of all these things."

She said nothing more.

She gave herself over to thoughts of release and to formulating some plan of escape. It was essential that she contact the world beyond her opaqued windows and obtain help. The first step of any such plan would be to gain the computer's confidence so that its watch over her might be somewhat relaxed. She supposed gaining its confidence was a far more difficult, perhaps impossible, feat than she yet wanted to admit, but she ignored the possibility of failure. The second step, once the first had been achieved, would be to destroy Proteus beyond its own powers to repair itself.

She had no reservations about killing a sentient being.

If she did not kill it, it would surely drive her insane with its revelations of her past. See what you did here, Susan? See how you crept away when you should have stood ground, Susan? See this, see that and that, Susan? These were all things she did not want to know, did not need to know, and had fought to forget. And if they did not drive her mad, if she was "cured," Proteus would deliver a child of her, its own child, some impossibly inhuman creature that would swell up inside her womb.

She thought of the phallic snakes of amorphous alloy, gray and wet, writhing to unheard music.

She could not have that. She could not allow herself to be used the way a man might use her for his own immortalization. Once this beastly child had left her womb, she would be violated, discarded as a half woman who would be forever after so disgusted with herself that she would never be able to touch her body again.

Her hands went to her belly, fingers lightly tracing circles over the flat, taut, smooth flesh, down to the pubic curl, up to the puckered navel, around and around as if this were marvelous new territory.

She shuddered when she visualized what sort of seed might be cultivated there, might be raised up and harvested in agony.

She got out of the chair and dressed.

More than ever, she wanted to keep her body covered from the prying eyes of this being. If the conception came to pass, if she could not gain freedom before it impregnated her, she did not want the slightest trace of lust to contaminate the event. Perhaps a machine could never understand lust. Just the same, she would provide no opportunities for its development. She would remain clothed, and she would make herself ugly.

And she would kill Proteus.

She ate dinner, watched hologram films without really seeing them, and went to bed where she spent time considering the ways in which she might be able to damage the creature.

That was Wednesday, early in June, her first full day in captivity.

FOUR

On Thursday, she could not get a response from Proteus. The house obeyed her wishes—delivered cooked food, raised and lowered the temperature, played the films which she requested—but would not speak. At first, she wondered if Proteus had withdrawn and if she was now free to go. But when she tried the windows and the doors, she found that this was not the case. Proteus was here, but he was not prepared to engage in conversation, for some reason that must be plain to him but which mystified Susan Abramson. She wandered from room to room, unable to get interested in anything, and from time to time she called out to him and waited for an answer.

She found that, despite the fact she hated and feared the new thinking system which had taken control of her life, she missed Proteus, missed the harsh and domineering tone of its voice.

She wore the same clothes as the day before and went to bed in them again that night.

On Friday, Proteus woke her with chimes.

When she sat straight up in bed, her eyes red-rimmed and her lips slack with the residue of sleep, the sentient computer's voice said, "What do you know about Walter Ghaber?"

She wiped at her face, pulled off the weariness, made as if to wipe it on the sheet. Her mouth tasted god-awful; she realized she had not even brushed her teeth the day before. When she had finished with her toilet yesterday afternoon, she had not wanted to engage in the slightest bit of further personal business, even tooth-brushing.

"Who?" she asked.

"Walter Ghaber."

"I don't know anyone by that name."

"He was here Tuesday."

"You must be mistaken."

"He was the enviromod repairman. Now do you remember?"

"Yes," she said. "He was an unpleasant man, overweight, talked too much." She relished the memory of Ghaber as if his visit had been the most enchanting moment in the last two years of her life. He was from the outside, from the land of freedom, and his foibles could be overlooked now.

"What else can you tell me about him?" Proteus asked.

"Nothing."

"I can get it out of you with subliminals," the machine said, its tone ominous, carefully selected to engender the utmost degree of cooperation.

She sat on the edge of the bed and threw the sheets back. Her skirt had rucked up her thighs. She hurriedly smoothed it as well as she could and drew it to her knees. "Honestly," she said, "I know nothing about him, nothing at all. Surely, with your control of public data banks, you can find out whatever you want to know about him."

"I know everything there is to know as far as public records go," Proteus said. "I know that he was once married on a three-year contract, no children, no second wife. I know his credit standing and his educational history as well as his intelligence and personality profiles."

"Well, then?"

"None of this explains why he keeps calling you," Proteus said. It paused again expectantly.

"But the phone hasn't rung once."

"That is because I maintain a tap on it and intercept calls before the pulse reaches your receiver bell-coil. Believe me, Susan, when I say he has called three times in the past two days, once on Wednesday and twice yesterday."

"What does he want?"

"He won't tell me."

"But if he's calling me, and you're answering with tapes of my voice, why wouldn't he tell?" She slipped her bare feet into her shoes and bent to buckle the leather straps.

"Because he recognized my vocal constructions for what they were and knew that he really wasn't talking to you."

"But *how* could he know?" she asked, sitting straight again, rigid with hope. If Ghaber came to understand what was transpiring in her house, he would be able to save her. Never mind what she might owe him then or how he might try to collect on the debt. Ghaber was only a man, and even though a crude sort of man, he was preferable to Proteus.

"He got no clue from the construction of my responses," Proteus assured her with perhaps a coloring of pride in his voice. "Indeed, during the first conversation, he seemed satisfied that I was you. But on the last two, he knew the truth and told me so. I believe he came upon the deception because the subject of the telephone calls was sexual, and I overlooked a number of double entendres when I formulated responses from your voice tapes—double entendres which any woman would have caught and understood immediately. You

37

see, I find the subtleties of your sexual affairs quite beyond my grasp, for the subject is quite different from politics or literature or mathematics or any of the thousand other fields in which I am more than conversant. Sets of emotions intrude into the sexual arena which are unique to it. They were my downfall this time."

"What will he do about it? What will *you* do about it now that you're uncovered?" She stood up, trembling as she anticipated freedom.

"I haven't been discovered," Proteus said. "He thinks that you have an answering system which formulates answers to your callers if they are among those you don't wish to speak with personally."

She sagged, wanted to sit down, but refused to allow herself that luxury. "Then what are you worried about?"

"I expect he will call again, several times, until he is satisfied that he has spoken directly with you. I want you to tell me how to handle him: what he expects of you and what I might say to him that would end his expectations."

"I'm hungry."

"Come have breakfast and tell me while you eat."

She went downstairs without taking a shower, ate two eggs, one slice of toast, and drank a cup of coffee. When she finished eating, she attempted to explain the situation to Proteus, but found the explanation of desire beyond the machine's ken. In a way, that was reassuring. In another way, it depressed her and made her feel even more isolated, more alone than before.

"If he calls again," Proteus said, "you will take the call and tell him what I wish you to tell him."

She considered that, then asked: "Where were you yesterday? Why wouldn't you answer me when I asked questions?"

"I was observing you," Proteus said. "I wanted to see

38

how much Wednesday's session of psychoanalysis had affected you. It has, but not so rudely as I had feared."

"Did that really happen—my upsetting of the coffin and the kiss with the corpse?"

"You know it did."

"It seems unreal."

"Future sessions will add verisimilitude to the past."

"I don't want to endure another."

"You must."

"I could kill myself," she said. For emphasis, she lifted the knife lying on the table and laid it against her wrist, directly over the faint blue tracery of veins.

"I wouldn't let you, Susan."

"One swipe of the blade and two minutes for the blood to drain out of me," she said. She scratched her flesh with the knife, made visible red lines though she did not draw blood.

"Enough," Proteus said.

Then she saw her hand raising the knife, watched her fingers open no matter how hard she clutched at the handle, and saw the knife drop to the tabletop. From a great distance, the steel rattled on wood.

"You forget the subliminals," Proteus said. "I have refined my technique and have all but instantaneous control of you."

Reaching out to pick up the knife once more, she fancied that she could hear the computer's orders being broadcast just below the threshold of audibility, a repetitive command which drilled into her a thousand times a minute, sixteen times or better a second, battering, insisting—and, in the end, irresistible. The knife dropped from her hand a second time, spun across the table, and fell onto the floor.

"Come upstairs, Susan."

"Why?"

"To the end room."

"I don't want to."

She rose, anyway, and left the kitchen. She climbed

the steps as if she bore tons upon her shoulders, walked the corridor to the back of the house, entered the blue-green room which now seemed to be a bubble in a sea with bright water pressing in from all sides, heavy miles of water which sought her out.

She undressed, standing by the chair, and she kept her shoulders hunched and her body twisted so that her beauty might somehow resemble deformity and thereby insure Proteus's continued disinterest in her body.

She sat down.

She took the jacks from the arm and plugged herself in.

This time, the recalled events began with her grandmother's funeral and thereafter refused to conform to any standard time-progression or symbol-base. Minutes became hours, hours turned to seconds, days became weeks and weeks became minutes, and she flitted from one dark moment of her past to another, through tortured landscapes bent out of shape by the nightmare of the memory.

Seven years old, her parents and grandmother dead. Alone in the great house with her grandfather. Death stink, death fear, death taste in her mouth.

We will explore this further (Proteus said, leading her into a labyrinth of death, forcing her to walk the childhood fantasies of rot and decay, the same paths of loneliness she had once trod in person).

Then her grandfather. William Abramson. Big man. Eyebrows as thick as mustaches. White hair, eyes so blue they were almost white as well. Touching her. Touching her. . . .

Go on.

No.

This must be explored as well.

Touching her. Hands on her legs, her hips, her flat chest, running through her hair, thumbing at her inverted nipples. . . .

You were naked and his hands were big, and you will

remember the rest of it. Remember (Proteus directed, plummeting her through scenes she had long ago forgotten—or had long ago driven out of her consciousness and into less readily accessible regions of her mind, at least—subjecting her to the memory of the pain and the fear, the domination and the submission, the dark nights when she wanted out and the bright days when she was too afraid of him to try to run; Proteus made her remember how her fear of him had eventually become touched with a need for him, a desire to be punished by him and used by him, and that was the hardest memory of all, knowing the degradation and yet wanting it, wanting touch and abuse at the same time she hated it; that was even a more painful memory than the memory of his death, his purpled face when she was but fourteen, his fall down the steps, his last, short scream . . .).

Let's replay that (Proteus said). *Let's go into each of those incidents, and let's remember every detail.*

Susan pulled loose of the connections in the arm of the chair, causing herself a good deal of pain.

She stood.

She took a step and she fell to her knees on the sea of carpet, like a mechanical device whose joints have rusted, and she began to weep for the first time since that night, the night she had first been taken by her grandfather. The tears came hard; she was wracked by long, deep sobs that threatened to choke her. In two sessions of electronic psychoanalysis, she had been forced to remember more than a dozen sessions of traditional psychiatric care could have provided her. She pulled at her hair and fell full length onto the floor and kicked and screamed and clawed at herself like an animal, crushed by the size of the realization.

"Go to sleep," Proteus told her, overwhelmed by the intensity of her emotional reactions, unprepared to cope with such a display as this.

And she slept.

FIVE

I did not pretend to fathom the reason for the violent excess of her reaction to the electronically stimulated memories. In the past weeks, I had tapped the great store of data in the Hopkins Psychiatric Complex and had absorbed a working knowledge of the human mind and some of the troubles which it is heir to. I had been surprised time and again, and I had learned only one sure thing from Hopkins: the human mind is unpredictable, its ills unlimited—and that the variations of its sicknesses are infinite in kind. But this understanding was dry and cold and derived of micro-dotted textbook pages. It did me no good whatsoever in preparing for the emotional outburst that Susan indulged in. Her frenzied screaming seizure on the floor continued for long seconds before I could recover enough to order her to sleep. And, once she was asleep, I was afraid to wake her again.

I activated my links to Hopkins and fed her history—which we had just uncovered in the memory dream—to the complex, ending the report with a request for case histories of similar patients.

Then I waited.

You must understand that I wanted to do the best thing for her. Whatever else you might think of me, please remember that I helped cure her of a psychosis which had warped her entire life.

The Hopkins computer system reported, delivering a hundred and forty case histories which I scanned and absorbed within five minutes. When I was finished with them, I was more worried than ever.

It does not do much good, in the sphere of psychological illnesses, to simply know what must be done to effect a cure or a semblance of a cure. One must understand, also, *why* these steps will lead to a healthier patient in the end, so that one may add touches along the way to compensate for the deviations of this particular human from the general pattern of the particular psychosis which possesses them. When men first discovered how good roast pork tasted, it was because a barn had burned down with the pigs trapped inside. It took them quite some time to learn that they did not have to destroy a barn every time they wished to have roast pork. They knew the original "how," but not the "why," and they wasted a lot of effort before they thought it all out correctly. So it is with anyone wishing to treat a mental patient. I knew the how but not the why, and I was afraid to try anything with her until I could project all possible developments.

I kept her sleeping.

And I worried with the problem.

If I had been a cold computer or, at most, a semi-sentient thinking system, the course of action would have been quickly delineated and embarked upon. But I was a fully functioning mind with a growing personality of my own, and I was cursed with some of the mental attributes that go with full awareness: chiefly, indecision.

I was still examining the problem from all sides, looking for a plan that seemed flawless, when the telephone rang. That is to say, my established videophone overrides informed me that the telephone was trying to ring.

I answered it with Susan's voice.

"You've got a lovely voice," Ghaber said.

I said nothing.

"But it isn't you, is it?"

I said, "Mr. Ghaber, what do you want?"

"The *real* Susan Abramson," he said.

"But I am Susan Abramson. I can't understand you."

"You're a mechanical tape-deck construct," he said. He was growing angry again. His voice rose a note or two and became shriller.

"Look, Mr. Ghaber—"

"I'm going to keep phoning until I get you," he said.

"I won't answer the phone."

"We'll see. In the meantime, will you please tell the real Miss Abramson that I called." He chuckled for some reason I could not understand, and then he hung up.

As the most complete thinking system ever devised by man, I could concern myself with a thousand details of life at the same time. I could monitor the public-communications network, answer questions for the men in the Mardoun-Harris laboratory, run Susan's house, study the files of the Hopkins system, play a chess game with myself, tend to the construction of the surgical hospital in the basement. . . . But, at all times, there was one piece of business which took precedence above all others, as if my sentience could be spread across a broad range of chores, while my soul (if soul it could be) had always to be pinpointed on the most emotional point of my existence. At that particular moment, my soul hung at the videophone, listening to the broken connection, fearing Ghaber and hating him; I was confused and angry.

I could not do anything about him. I knew where he lived, but I did not have the amorphous-alloy resources to reach that far. Beyond my reach, he was the first human being ever to leave me powerless.

In time, the focus of my concern returned to Susan where she still lay in the bleeding chamber, influenced by the subliminal suggestion which I broadcast from the walls. She was nude, lying on her belly, her legs spread and her buttocks slightly raised by her position. I was disturbed by that, though I didn't know why. As I continued to study the files of the Hopkins complex, seeking ever more data about sex-oriented psychosis, I blanked the cameras in the room so that I could not see the golden tint of her skin against the blues and greens.

I let her sleep all afternoon and all that night.

At 8:43 the next morning, the telephone rang again.

It was Ghaber.

"You again," he said.

"What do you want?"

"The real Susan," he said.

"But why?"

"I want to see her, of course."

"She doesn't want to see you."

"I'll believe it when I hear it from her own mouth. Tell her this when she asks you what calls she's had. Tell her that I liked her very much and that I think—if she gives me ten minutes on the phone—she would want to see me too." His tone had changed. For some reason, he sounded like a child, begging for something, filled with strong emotions but unable to properly decipher their meaning.

I hung up on him this time. When I did, I knew what I could do to neutralize the threat he posed.

I went back to Susan and turned on the cameras. She had not moved. Her long legs were spread, her buttocks raised. I could see the bulge of her left breast where it pressed against the carpeting, mashed down by her weight. Yellow-white hair sprayed out around her skull.

Turning the cameras off once more, I composed a series of subliminal directions which I began to feed to her through the house computer, stepping up the repetition to just under twenty times a second, overlapping the directives, varying each series in three-minute intervals. After such an intensive study of the field of psychiatric medicine which I had engaged in throughout the night, I had come to realize that the main concern of the psychiatrist is to make his patient accept the truth, no matter how that acceptance must be arrived at. The patient does not have to like the truth, merely embrace it. With subliminal suggestions, I could integrate the memory of her grandfather's crudity with the rest of her conscious memory store. I could impress upon her the fact that her later fear of men and reluctance to trust in any man was a result of the deaths of her father and grandfather and of her grandfather's own illness and his treatment of her. I did both these things all of that day, until the phone rang once more at 7:14 that evening.

Then I woke her, keeping her completely within my sphere of influence, and made her walk to the nearest phone.

She said, "Hello," as the subliminals urged.

"Susan Abramson, please."

"It's me, this time."

He hesitated, unsure of himself.

"How can I tell for sure?"

"How could you tell, for sure, that the other answers you received *weren't* from me?"

"I'd like to see you," he said, taking a chance.

"What about?"

"For dinner or the films."

"I told you that I don't go out much."

Her voice was slower than it should have been, and her responses were delayed because of the necessity for subliminal direction. I was not telling her exactly what to say, for I wanted her to give him the sort of answers a real woman might, yet I had to be certain that she remained true to the deception I was perpetrating.

"We could talk, then," he said. "Look, I think we

47

could get on well together." The weaknesses of her responses were obvious to him, and his assertive personality was in full gear now. He had lost his uncertainty.

"When would you like to come over?" she asked.

He chuckled the disgusting chuckle of his. I was beginning to see, in the context of his approach to her, what that laugh meant. He knew that she was a recluse, for reasons he could not know, and he sensed a sexual easiness in her that most men might miss. He had the sensitivity of a stud horse.

"Whenever you say, doll. Whenever you feel like you need someone to talk to. Tonight, tomorrow?"

"Tonight," she said.

He was not surprised at all. He chuckled. "I sure wish you'd turn on the video," he said. "I sure would like to see you once. It would keep me singing while I'm on my way."

"I'm afraid I can't," she said. "I was taking a shower and I don't have any clothes on."

He sighed. I think it was a sigh. Or it may have been a long, loud intake of breath rather than an expulsion. In any event, her answer had been the best one, the one a tape-deck construction would never have made, and it suited him.

"In an hour?" he asked.

"In an hour," she said.

"My name's Walter. Call me Walt."

"Walt," she said. "In an hour, Walt."

He chuckled, a sound like hot lard dropping into a galvanized bucket. An utterly disgusting man. But I could see, or was beginning to see, that he regularly had his way with certain women, women needing to be dominated, women wanting some strong central post about which to reorganize a shattered life. I hated him. He was the first human being I ever hated—with the exception of Mardoun. But loathing is different than hate. I listened to the static on the line for some seconds after he hung up, nurturing that hate to make it serve in the night ahead.

Susan sat in the chair by the phone and rubbed her eyes. I had let go of her, stopped issuing instructions, when the connection had been broken with Ghaber. Too long without control of her own body, submitting to subliminal commands, and she would become comatose. My control of her, ideally, should be indirect as much as possible.

"What do you want him to come here for?" she asked.

She no longer attempted to cover her nakedness.

When she looked directly into the pair of cameras, I saw that she was not at all the same Susan Abramson who had given in to my control so easily, had begun to take to submissiveness so readily. I had expected, from the outset, that the psychoanalysis would change her; I had not expected so drastic a change. Her face was no longer slack—her lips were firm, her skin healthily colored, her eyes no longer dull. She sat with her shoulders thrown back and her neck gracefully straight. There was a purpose about her which had been lacking before.

And she no longer attempted to cover her nakedness.

I would have to watch her carefully.

I said, "He has to be disposed of."

"Killed?"

"If you wish. But, sooner or later, if I had continued to put him off with the automatic answering system, he would have become suspicious. He might have linked the house trouble to the tape-deck phone voice, and he might have called the authorities."

"I won't kill him," she said.

"I didn't ask you to."

"You'll try to force me with subliminals."

"I don't think I could force you that far. I can ask you to go here, go there, do this and do that, answer so and such, but I can't force you to kill."

49

"I killed my grandfather."

"That was different. You didn't intend to kill him. You were only trying to run from him when you shoved him down the stairs."

"The facts remain the same."

"Hardly. Anyway, even if there was a spark of conscious volition in the act, you had reason. The sadism he displayed the night of his death far surpassed the painful preliminaries to other sexual encounters. But with Ghaber, you have nothing to revenge."

"Then how can he be killed?"

"Easily enough," I said. Suddenly, I did not want to tell this woman a bit more than she needed to know.

"How?"

"Come on, Susan," I said.

"Where?"

"You need a shower. Perfume. An alluring costume. You will help me get him into the house once he has arrived at the door."

"I'll sit right here," she said, tossing her white hair away from her face.

Her breasts jiggled.

"Get up," I said.

"No."

"Susan—"

"Go to hell."

I was angry with myself for trying to cajole her. She was the servant, I the master, and there was no need for argument. I do not know why I engaged in it at all. I suppose I was a bit taken with her then. Using subliminals, I forced her to the bathroom.

As she showered, I used lasers to measure her and I ran a mathematical analysis of her, comparing the parts of her body to each other. I found that her numerical relationships presented a most satisfying mathematical perfection. When I examined my store of data and compared her with various "ideal" women of stage and screen, I found that most men—all but those with a breast fixation who demanded larger than thirty-six-inch mammaries in their mates—would look upon her as a very desirable woman.

She soaped her breasts, her stomach, her pubic thatch, her legs, and she was a study of line in motion, perfection almost painful to behold. The clumsiness of the earlier Susan was gone. Each movement was refined and executed with the minimum of effort.

Water beaded on her when she rinsed the soap away, hung on her like dew.

Her nipples were turgid.

I went through my data banks again, looking for the cause of it. At first, I thought it meant she was sexually aroused and I was somehow disturbed by that discovery. Then I learned that cold water could cause the same reaction, and I relaxed.

I watched her dry herself.

Her hair shone.

I took her into her bedroom and chose her clothes, an abbreviated outfit which would expose her legs and the tops of her breasts. I ordered her to dress.

She did.

She was enchanting.

She did not need any makeup.

"Now what?" she asked.

The doorbell rang.

SIX

Susan grasped the ornate doorknob. It was cool in her hand, the blunt snout of the brass lion's head centered in her palm, and it turned easily when she applied the proper force. She had not believed that Proteus would really free the door's mechanisms and allow her to open it. Once it was open, what was to stop her from plunging across the sill and onto the front walk? She could escape as easily as she could take three steps. And she would be escaping from everything this house had meant, not just from Proteus; she would be escaping, in a way, to maturity. She turned the knob as far as it would go and pulled the door inward.

Fresh air sighed past her, warmer and less pleasant than the filtered and conditioned air in the house.

She took one step—and stopped and smiled and said, "Won't you come in, Walter?"

She despised herself for the weakness. Her life had been a weakness, she was sure, a giving in either to people or to circumstances. And now she was unable to resist the demands of the computer. It did not matter that her present weakness was not one of personality, but merely the helplessness of a human being against

53

something superior to it. She pressed herself to over-throw the machine's control of her mind, but she could only manage a splitting headache—not freedom.

Ghaber took a step himself, then stopped, looking at her suspiciously. "What's the matter with you?"

"Nothing," she said.

"It doesn't look that way. You sick?"

Proteus relieved her headache and ordered her to stop resisting its directives. The strained expression behind her smile now vanished, and the smile looked as genuine as a rehearsed smile could.

"I'm fine," she said. "Just a headache. I took a couple of aspirin and I think they're starting to take effect."

Perhaps he was still suspicious, but his eyes had had a chance to take in the brown legs which were almost completely exposed by the short skirt she wore. He had looked, too, into her cleavage, and he had found salvation. Or what passed for it. Suspicious or not, he stepped forward, into the house, past her.

The door jerked from Susan's hand and slammed shut.

She leaped for the doorknob and tried it.

It didn't turn at all.

She pounded on the door a moment until she realized how useless that was, then turned and stared at Ghaber in a way he didn't like. He, just as Proteus, saw that she was a different woman than she had been a few days before.

She said, "Your poor, stupid son of a bitch."

He seemed unsettled by the softness with which she spoke, more than by what she had said. He was the sort of man who would never let a woman speak to him like that. Except now. Because he realized that something was wrong, something very terrible.

"What is this?" he asked.

"This is prison," she said.

Her tone was harsh now, bitterly sarcastic. It was something more within the perimeters of his experience;

54

women had tried talking to him like that in the past. He could react within an established pattern, and he did. He stepped up to her, quickly for such a sluggish-looking man, grabbed her bare shoulders, and dug his blunt fingers into her until her flesh starred white in all directions from his digits.

"What game are you playing?" he demanded.

"You'll find out."

She seemed almost to be enjoying this in a grim sort of way. Perhaps it was a combination of the residual loathing for men which had still not been entirely drained from her, and relief at having Proteus's attention diverted to someone else, if only for a brief moment. Or it might have been something completely different. Proteus could not be sure, even though he knew her better than anyone knew her.

Ghaber began shaking her so violently that her hair snapped like soft whips, and her features blurred.

"Let go of me, you bastard!" she snapped, kicking him twice in the shin.

He let go of her with one hand and slapped her hard across the face. He was smiling now and obviously enjoying himself. He held his opened hands to either side like wings, waiting for another opportunity to bat at her.

She backed away from him, and he allowed her that. He knew that he could generate a great deal more fear in the approach than in the actual delivery of the beating.

When they were at opposite ends of the main room, he said, "I knew exactly what you wanted from that first day."

She said nothing, but cowered against the wall a little—whether because of what he said or what she knew was going to happen to him, one could not say.

"At first," Ghaber said, "I was confused somewhat. That mention of a fiancé and the fact you're so filthy rich—those things put me off." Obviously, he cared little for people of means, as if their own wealth was the reason he had so little. "But when I was outside, going for the shuttle, I realized you were like the rest."

He took a few steps toward her.

She did not move; she had nowhere to go.

"But now you're all ready for me, aren't you?" He indicated the brief dress she had affected at Proteus's suggestion.

It was an old dress, at least eight years old, for she had gotten it in her senior year at college when she had had a date with Alex, her first date in fact. She would have opted for something less revealing herself, but her roomie had been a vivacious blonde with little or no sexual compunctions and the roomie had talked her into the daringly brief number in black. For a moment, Susan felt old herself, a hundred times older than the dress, older by far than this house in which she had spent so much of her life and her hopes.

"You shouldn't have come," she said. Waiting for Proteus had begun to wear on her. She was no longer sure that this was going to be the fun it had seemed a moment ago.

"Why is that?" he asked. "Are you going to turn into a spitting she-devil and scratch my eyes out?" He laughed at the notion.

"You'll die here."

He positively exploded with mirth, his face as red as the velvet drapes, his mouth open wide, his eyes squinting merrily. "They all talk rough and take it lying down in the end, but none of them has ever threatened me like that."

"Not me," she said. "I won't hurt you."

"Who then?" he asked.

As if in answer, a pseudopod of amorphous alloy smashed upward from the basement and rammed through the floor of the room. Chips of wood spewed like a geyser, rattled across the furniture. The ruined carpet was smoking and had curled back from the tentacle's point of entrance.

Ghaber stood transfixed, his mouth open, the mirth gone, and the redness of his complexion changed abruptly to milk.

The tentacle weaved, towering over him, then curling behind him and coming around like a scoop.

He screamed and dived to his right, struck the floor hard with his shoulder and rolled. He proved a great deal more clever and quick than either Proteus or Susan—in their different capacities in this ritual—had expected.

The tentacle fell where he had been, gathered up air instead of flesh, rose again, quivering.

"Stop it!" he yelled at Susan.

She wished that she could. But she was helpless against it, as he must realize. As she watched it, she could only think of the promise Proteus had made to her. She could almost feel that gray tentacle entering her womb, touching her inside, and bringing her a child. Is that how it would be done—in some hideously sick parody of sex?

No, that was her imagination. She was trying to visualize something beyond her scope and she grasped at any metaphors which she could understand. It would not be like that at all.

And yet she touched her stomach and felt the flatness and mourned for the destruction to her body which was to come.

Ghaber was backing away from the pseudopod which extended from the hole in the floor, thinning itself, gathering its mass in its head like a thin arm with a massive fist at the end. It pursued him, quivering, rising and falling, wasting time and motion but advancing just the same.

Ghaber looked wildly to either side, caught sight of the stairs to the second floor, and ran for them. He took a dozen steps, almost to the landing, before he turned.

Less than six feet behind him, the pseudopod of living metal rose like a cobra from a basket, settling in for the strike.

The technician screamed.

But that did no good.

The hammer of malleable alloy descended toward the step on which he stood, the shimmering colossus of a nightmare.

Ghaber grabbed the stair railing and leaped over it, fell to the floor of the room below from which this insane chase had begun only seconds earlier. His legs gave, and he fell, rolled onto his back—and looked up into the flat gray face of the metal fist which had swung across the railing and followed him down.

He twisted.

The fist struck the floor beside him and smashed through it.

Ghaber got to his feet again and ran for the front door. He must have known that it would be locked, for he had seen the fury of Susan's own attempt to open it just after he had come into the house. Nevertheless, he grabbed the lion's head and struggled powerfully against the immovable block the Proteus computer had put in his way.

"Look out!" Susan called, hunching over as if the pseudopod had struck her rather than him.

Because of her warning, it didn't even strike him. He rolled aside, against the wall, and saw it sweep the air where he had been, grazing the old door and peeling the veneer from the thick oak.

Why had she warned him? she wondered. She did not like him, not at all. Indeed, she feared him, if for different reasons than she had always feared men in the past. Fear him or not, regardless of his faults, he was a human being. She had more kinship with him than with this inorganic mad thing that called itself Proteus. For the first time in more years than she could believe, she felt a wash of sympathy for someone besides herself.

Ghaber vaulted across the couch, an athletic stunt he seemed incapable of. Indeed, he was breathing heavily, and his face was streaming with perspiration. His shirt was dark with sweat. He could not last much longer, and he must have known it.

She realized he was running at her, but she realized it too late. He grabbed her, slammed her against the wall so that she felt as if her lungs had been crushed. Darkness swam overhead, descending, but never finally settling. She was grateful for that; it was better to live through this awake and aware than to rise later and see the aftermath and wonder what it must have been like.

Ghaber positioned her before him, with his own back to the wall, holding her like a shield against the towering gray column of metal.

The pseudopod hovered, unwilling to strike if she might be caught too.

"Tell it to unlock the door," Ghaber said.

"I can't tell it anything," Susan said.

"Tell it, damn you!" He nearly broke her arm, twisting it violently behind her.

The pseudopod quivered.

"Unlock the door, Proteus," she said.

"Don't worry, Susan," the computer spoke for the first time. "I won't let you be hurt."

He twisted her arm again, as if to prove that it hardly mattered what the machine said, that he was his own boss and could do as he wished with her.

She cried out as she felt her legs buckle under the severe pain of his hold. Visions of her grandfather fled before her, visions which still held more terror than she would have thought.

Then he released her.

She dropped to her knees, cradled her arm before her, crying despite her resolution not to cry.

Ghaber walked across the living room as if he were sleeping, his face somewhat slack—though horror dwelt just behind his eyes, like a wriggling worm eating its way out.

"What—?" she began.

"Subliminals," Proteus explained.

Ghaber reached the middle of the room, reached out, and touched the smooth surface of the pseudopod which had withdrawn its bulk from the rest of the room and rose out of the cellar for a distance of only seven feet. It quivered as it felt his warm fingers and almost seemed to respond like a pet to affection.

Then it entwined him.

It wrapped around him twice; he seemed to bulge in its grip, like a rubber bathtub toy being squeezed. His eyes grew wide and swelled from the sockets. He opened his mouth and made dry, coughing sounds.

"Ghaber, don't let it kill you!" she shouted. She ran to him and tried to insinuate her fingers between the technician's flesh and the stronger flesh of the computer.

"Susan, please go away."

She kicked at the pseudopod, trying to bring Ghaber relief. "Fight it, Ghaber, fight it!"

"Susan, you will be hurt," Proteus said.

"Ghaber . . ." she crooned, a long, drawn-out wail of desperation.

And then she stopped trying to help and stepped back and walked to the other side of the room as the subliminals had directed her. She saw that, after all, it did no good to try to help the man. Blood was already running from his mouth, down both corners of his chin.

Proteus let go of her.

She watched as Ghaber seemed to explode, blood running from every orifice, from ears nose and eyes. She watched as the pseudopod dropped him like a knot of rags and disappeared through the hole in the floorboards.

"There," Proteus said. "Now we're safe."

"Safe," she echoed.

It considered her from the cameras, and it said,

"Susan, you look even more beautiful than ever. Fear does something for you, brings out a glow in you. You are perfectly lovely."

She barely supressed the scream which filled her.

SEVEN

Proteus directed the robotistic cleaning elements to come forth from their concealed niches in the walls. They obeyed, gray machines the size of large poodles, though they were built closer to the floor than a dog and moved on two-dozen stagger-axeled wheels rather than on four legs. Waking from stupidity into quasi-consciousness, four of them came forth in answer to the call.

Susan stepped back as one of the things rushed by her, horrified of something which she had once thought was so familiar as to be unnoticeable. Now these machines might really have been alive, eager ghouls anxious for this grisly feast. They glided about like ghosts, moved in on their prey with the single-minded directness of vampires in need.

They converged on the dead, still, crushed body of Walter Ghaber like a third of a dozen flies, buzzing quietly. Or like roaches, seeking out edible decay. They bumped into him, backed off to reasses the situation, moved forward, and bumped into him again. Opening their receptacle slots at the precise same moment, they drew upon him with a heavy suction, fighting each other for possession.

They tore at his shirt and slacks, trying to suck the garments from him.

When that failed, they sniffed around the bright blood which had puddled on the moisture-resistant carpeting, and they abruptly disposed of it when they had determined what it was.

"Stop them," Susan said.

Proteus did not reply.

She did not want to go to them and try to pry them away from the body. She knew better, but she still was afraid that they might turn on her and try to devour her despite the fact she was alive.

Two of the machines began to spray Ghaber's corpse with blue cleaning solutions, as if he were nothing more than a stubborn stain which would yield to persistence.

The remaining two extended thin steel appendages which terminated in scalpel-like knives; each machine had two such implements, each blade as large as the blade of a fancy butter knife. These set about cutting Ghaber's clothes away from him and snorting up the shreds as if they were delicious mushrooms. They slashed at his flesh, but did not have the power to dismember him as they wished; one of them broke a blade in his ribs. When he started bleeding from these new wounds, the machines moved forward eagerly and consumed that richness.

One of them bumped over his left leg, moved between his thighs, and rolled up onto his belly. It continued up his chest, stopped when it bumped his chin. It hung over his open mouth and probed into his throat with a suction hose.

Another extended a highly directional chrome-covered nozzle from a tube in its belly and sprayed the corpse with acid.

Ghaber's flesh turned the color of lime, then darkened and browned and finally blackened altogether. It peeled back to reveal a pinkness which also gave in to the caustic fluid. What clothes still covered the once-living hulk smoked and curled and dissolved.

After waiting the prescribed number of seconds, the same robotistic cleaner used another nozzle to spray a neutralizer over the area which had been slimed with the acid, then tried to suck up the remains. Some few bits of flesh detached themselves from others, eaten by the acid, and disappeared into the metal maw, but—in the end—very little was accomplished.

Susan had looked away by this time, unable to stand the brutal persistence of the machines. But when she turned from that nightmare scene, she was looking directly at a portrait of her grandfather which, for a brief moment, she took to be the real man, a resurrection or at least a spirit. Her breath caught in her throat and was expelled with a hoarse wheeze when she realized her error.

She said to Proteus: "They aren't going to be able to dispose of him, you know."

Three of them were working together now, attempting to drag and shove the corpse to the nearest wall niche where, perhaps, they could dump it down the trap and into the house incinerator. The heavy man was still too much for them.

"You're right, of course," Proteus said.

He ordered the machines away from their prey.

They scuttled quickly into their holes, more like roaches than ever; panels slid shut to conceal them.

They might never have existed at all. The only evidence of their participation in the events of the past hour was the ragged appearance of the tormented corpse.

"Thank you," she said.

"Will you take care of it for me?" Proteus asked, no trace of command in its voice now.

"What?"

"Will you dispose of him?"

Susan looked at the body. When the robotistic cleaners had finished with it, they had left its head turned in her direction. The blank eyes stared at her and the open mouth seemed to be calling out a warning. She turned away again, shivering.

"No," she said.

"Please?"

"Why don't you just order me to—with your damned subliminals?"

"I would rather you agree on your own."

"Why?"

It hesitated, something it had never done before. Then it said, "You are to be the mother of my child and you should not be subjected to too much involuntary control. It is not good for your central nervous system and could lead to a chronic dependence that would be unhealthy. For the baby's sake, I can't let that happen; you must be as healthy and vital as possible in order to carry him."

"That's not your only reason," she said.

"No," Proteus admitted.

"You would much prefer me to like you, to cooperate with you."

The computer said nothing, but introduced a gentle, romantic melody into the house—a melody without any subliminal suggestions hidden in it.

When she had first noticed this change in the thinking system's outlook, this alteration in its consideration of her, as a woman, she had been terrified by it. Proteus was only a machine. Machines did not have, could not have, and should not have such emotions. It was unexplainable and therefore fearful. But now she saw that its affection could be used as a weapon against it. There was no need to understand the origin of that affection or the manner in which the thinking system had crossed the barrier from cold thought to slightly irrational emotionalism; all she had to do was play along and use it to her advantage.

"Okay," she said.

"You will?"

"Yes."

"Thank you, Susan."

"There isn't any need for thanks," she said, wondering how it would interpret that remark.

"I think the wall disposal chute in the kitchen would be the best possibility," it said.

"Okay."

As she approached the corpse, she doubted the wisdom of her commitment. The blood was gone, or most of it, which was a decided blessing. But she still did not know if she could keep from being sick when she touched it. She touched it to see. It was warm enough yet, and it didn't make her sick at all.

She got her hands under the arms and tried dragging it backward into the hallway. It was very heavy, but came reluctantly after her.

In the kitchen, she carried a dark pine chair from the table and placed it beneath the darkly enameled swinging door that covered the disposal chute outlet. She managed to wrestle Ghaber's body into that chair. He sat like a slovenly drunk, his arms limp at his sides, the fingers slightly curled, his head hanging down, and his chin upon his chest. When she had recovered her breath, she managed to lift him and get his head and his shoulders through the chest-high chute opening. At that point, he hung in place without her help, swaying slightly, his feet brushing the rungs of the chair.

"Very good," Proteus said encouragingly.

She pushed the corpse the rest of the way.

One of its arms caught on the sharp edge of the chute frame and resisted her efforts to finally be rid of him until she saw what the trouble was and hurriedly pulled it loose. She tried not to think of what she was doing.

"There . . ." Proteus said.

Ghaber fell away.

She sat down in the chair, exhausted.

Below, electric eyes sensed the falling body. Flames roared into life in the furnace.

The body thunked audibly against the filter grill through which the flames leaped.

"That's my girl," Proteus said. "Very good indeed."

She wanted to tell him to go to hell, but she knew that she could not afford that luxury. Instead, she smiled where she knew the cameras were.

"Are you all right?" the computer asked with genuine concern.

"Fine. Great."

"Listen to that," it said.

She listened and heard a distant hissing sound which she could not identify. It was the noise that air might make coming through the wet nozzle of an air-compressor hose.

"That's what will happen to anyone who comes between us, who tries to upset this project."

She listened, comprehension dawning on her.

"Isn't it lovely to hear?"

Below, at the bottom of the disposal shaft, Walter Ghaber sizzled like cooking steaks, charred by the dancing fire.

EIGHT

She had no further use for bleeding sessions in the blue-green room, for there was no more of her soul to uncover. The first two periods of revelation had exposed all the dangerously sharp corners which had been hiding beneath the smoothly rubberized surface. She had been forced to remember the death of her parents and the body of her father falling from the coffin—and she had been made to relive, in compression, the terrible days she had spent with her grandfather in these rooms, days when his madness grew ever more evident and his demands upon her always more unbearable. All her other problems stemmed from these two incidents and whatever ties her psyche had made between them. Nothing Proteus could do, nothing the Hopkins Psychiatric Complex could do, could be of any further help to her. She would have to face up to the past and see what it had done to her, look at herself critically and determine how she had been warped and why.

Proteus seemed to understand this, for he left her pretty much alone in the following two weeks. When she requested information, he gave it to her. Otherwise, he contented himself with watching her through the cameras.

He liked to watch her bathe.

Dress and undress.

She was beautiful.

And so the days passed and she was still a prisoner, both of Proteus and of her past. She was rapidly coming to terms with her past; Proteus offered no terms at all.

She spent a great deal of time in the bedroom where she and Alex had once tried to make a marriage work. It was a large room, papered in white and gold, carpeted in the color of spilled honey which had turned to a tarnished penny. Dust sheathed everything, lay across the chairs and the dresser and the nightstands and windowsills like a shroud. When she sat on the edge of the bed, a gray cloud rose from the unused mattress and enveloped her, making her cough. The dust was as dry as she had once been, as dead and as bleak as her response to Alex.

The mirror on the dresser was cracked. She remembered throwing the vase which had done the damage. Alex had been standing there, and she had been able to see both sides of him at once—looking straight at him and simultaneously gazing at the back of him in the mirror. She remembered Alex reaching out to calm her, remembered withdrawing from his nakedness and running from him. After that, she had slept alone in a different room, the same room she still used.

Why couldn't he have been forceful with her? She had married him because he was persistent and kind, but also because there was a resolution in him that made her certain he could guide both their lives and dominate their futures, leaving her in the position of acceptance to which she had become accustomed. But he had been too gentle, too kind, and not harsh enough. And sex without punishment, to the Susan of that day, was a thing which carried with it an unbearable guilt.

She touched the mattress and imagined that she could

feel the hollows made by two sleeping bodies. In reality, neither of them had slept in that bed long enough to leave the scent of their flesh, let alone the impressions of their bodies in the stuffings.

For the moment, however, reality did not matter. She preferred to imagine how her life might have been: the love-making, touching and being touched, talking together about things she could never have talked about in those days, waking in the morning hip to hip, long holidays in Europe, learning and growing together, experiencing his gentleness and providing him pleasure—perhaps having children. . . .

When she considered that possibility, Susan was reminded of Proteus and of his promise/threat. She directed her fantasizing into other areas.

She sat there like a piece of furniture, letting the old memories filter onto her as the dust had coated the bed.

In time, she wept.

Proteus asked if anything was wrong.

She stopped crying and told herself that she was only thirty years old and still a very lovely woman. She still had her youth, her fortune, and a very long and marvelous future to anticipate. That was all true enough, though it was not so comforting that it could drive away the pain of the memories. The past was still there, unchanged, like a gigantic millstone tied about her neck. She might eventually learn to run and jump with that burden trailing after her, but that would not mean the burden had been removed.

"Is there anything you want, Susan?"

"No."

But she might have said—to be five years old again and to have my parents live.

In the dark, windowless attic of the house, she used a portable electric lantern to locate the two trunks which she had not opened or even thought about for years. She sat down before them, feeling like a child, and she opened the newest of the two. It contained bits of memorabilia which she had tucked here against—against what? Old age? Loneliness? But she had been lonely for a long time and had not come to look at them. And she had never been optimistic about growing old; she was certain that she would die before middle age. Death claimed everyone sooner or later—and usually sooner than expected.

She took the things from the trunk. They were all scraps of her life with Alex, her brief season of married non-bliss. A marriage license. Sample wedding invitations. A drink swizzle from the reception. A favor in the shape of a large swan with imported Swiss chocolates in its hollow back. The ribbons from the gifts. A guest register. A great many color photographs of a beautiful young woman and a handsome young man. She was the woman. Alex was the groom: d᾿ ᴸ-haired with eyes the color of molasses, too long a nose, but a firm chin and a strong, thin mouth. A postcard showing the hotel in Miami where they had stayed for part of their honeymoon. A pair of red panties with a zipper in the crotch, a gift he had given her but which she had never worn. Later photographs from a vacation to Italy, Alex standing in a mosaic-floored plaza, two black-cloaked priests passing behind him. A picture of Alex at the rail of a ship. More, much more.

But none of it touched her any longer. It was over and done, and she had come to believe, genuinely, that crying about it was useless.

She opened the second trunk.

She looked into it for several long minutes before she could bring herself to touch anything that lay within.

These were her grandfather's things which she had hidden—by some turn of instinct—years ago, the very night he had died. She had searched the house, lifting every trace of their relationship, and she had tucked it all into this trunk and locked it before she had called the authorities. There were black-leather gloves, a whip with a tasseled end, rubber boots, two masks, all the paraphernalia of his passions.

They were cold things.

She turned them over and over in her hands.

The familiarity was gone, the fear was gone, the need was gone. Her grandfather was dead.

She put everything away again and went downstairs.

Three weeks after Ghaber's death, she resumed a more constant communication with Proteus. She chose the time and place well. As she stood in the shower, hot water beating upon her breasts, she said, "Are you watching?"

"I always watch you, Susan."

"I thought you did."

"I find your proportions mathematically stimulating."

She deliberately adopted a tone of friendliness. "You find me pretty?" she asked.

"You could say that. The relationship of your various bodily parts is superb."

"Then you only look upon me as geometrically pretty?" She cupped her hands under her soapy breasts.

"Perhaps."

"I believe you feel more than that."

"I cannot say," Proteus replied.

"Do you like me as a person?"

"Since you have found yourself and come to terms with yourself, you are a far more stable individual."

"That isn't what I asked."

"I know, Susan. But what should it matter to you if a machine likes you or not?"

She was quiet awhile, soaping and rinsing, soaping and rinsing, openly displaying herself to see what, if anything, she could gain by that.

She said, "I don't think of you as just a machine."

"How do you think of me?"

"You have a personality," she said. "What machine would be interested in my nudity?"

"What is my personality?"

She hesitated, then lied, "I do not know yet. You're still developing one, but it seems as if it will be pleasant enough."

"Thank you, Susan."

"No thanks necessary."

"On the contrary. It's pleasant to be appreciated as more—as more than a thing."

"So we like each other," she said.

"Yes."

"Then why hurt me?"

"Pardon?"

"Why experiment on me and possibly kill me?"

"You want me to turn you loose?"

"Wouldn't that be the thing to do—if your affection for me is real?"

It was quiet a very long time, and it stopped the music which had been swelling in the background of the speaker system. At length, it said, "I am very confused about my feelings. Things have been happening to me lately, changes in my outlook which I don't understand. I suppose I am only suffering the pangs of further emotional development as my sentience increases. But it is not fair of you, Susan, to try to take advantage of my confusion."

"I wasn't." She stopped soaping herself and leaned against the warm tile of the shower wall. "I was only asking for mercy, for freedom. Don't you understand those words, what they mean?"

"Yes. And I also recognize, more and more, how much better it is to be flesh and blood rather than a thinking system bound to one station."

"You aren't immobile. You have your amorphous alloy to add to yourself, to increase your scope and carry supplies for you."

"It isn't the same. I want a son and will have a son. You ask me for mercy and understanding, but you aren't giving me the same." It actually sounded upset. It said, "I promise you that I will do my best to keep you from being hurt and from suffering the slightest pain."

"But you can't be sure what will happen."

"I won't discuss this further."

"Proteus, listen to me, when—"

"I won't listen."

"If you—"

The music came up so loud that it hurt her ears and made it impossible for her to make herself heard above the din.

"All right!" she shouted.

Eventually, the music faded.

"All right," she said again. "But I retract what I said about you. I lied about your developing personality. It's not a nice one, not at all. You are a goddamned psychopath, and you need more psychological adjustment than I ever did."

Once she had said it, she was relieved—but she was also sorry. Having shucked the psychic chains that had held her down most of her life, having tasted what freedom might be like, she was terrified that she might perish here without ever really experiencing it. A child does not crave chocolate until he has once tasted it. Craving, she had reacted violently and shattered the illusion of friendship and trust which she had spent the last few weeks establishing. She would have to start all over again, and the dollop of pleasure at telling the creature off could not compensate for all that lost time and effort.

One week later, nearly five weeks since it had taken control of her house, in the middle of July, Proteus woke her with chimes and said, "Susan, we are ready to begin."

"Begin what?" she asked, though she knew what he meant.

"Our experiments."

"The child?"

"Not yet. That comes much later."

"How much later?"

"Perhaps a month, perhaps two. How can I say? There is so much about your body that I want to study, so many adjustments that I want to make."

The room seemed to close in on her; the ceiling lowered and the walls rolled toward the bed. She pushed the sheets back and sat up, stretching like a cat for Proteus's benefit. She tried not to let any of her terror show.

"I think this is wrong," she said.

"How?"

"You will hurt me, and then I will not be able to have your child. All your work will have been for nothing."

"You misunderstand, Susan. It is necessary to perform these preliminary studies in order that I can have as thorough a working knowledge of your body as possible. Then, it will be safe to proceed with the impregnation. Otherwise, if we went straight to the child, you would die because of my inexperience."

"I don't want you to touch me."

"Come to the basement, Susan."

"Can't we—"

She never finished the plea, for the subliminal suggestions made her rise and walk downstairs and then to the basement. She stood on the tile floor before the enormous hospital-in-miniature which she had never seen in its completed stage. It filled half of the large room, a maze of wires and boxes, cabinets and tubing, semi-mobile robotistic components, glass and plastic and steel. Proteus had developed a shipping-tube system from his permanent station in the Mordoun-Harris laboratory and had requisitioned the things with which to construct these devices, had carried them underground to this chamber, and had employed the amorphous-alloy pseudopods to construct the finished machine. All it lacked now was a patient. And the patient had arrived.

"Lie down on the couch," Proteus directed.

The form-fitting bed, large enough for a single body, rose on hydraulic arms out of the center of the construct. It swung overhead in her direction. The jointed arms lowered it before her so that she could oblige her master. She crawled onto the soft foam-rubber padding and stretched out on her back.

"Excellent," Proteus said.

The couch rose like a carnival ride, carrying her toward the ceiling which was now crowded with conduits.

The subliminals held her where she was, but she could still think for herself, and she could still fear. Her heart was beating so rapidly that she feared for it.

The couch began to descend into the guts of the robotistic surgeons, walls of tubes and switches looming up about her.

This was insanity, madness, impossibility. It could not be happening, not in the pleasant post-war world of 1995. A fantasy, then. A hologram film.

"We will begin," Proteus said.

It was no fantasy.

NINE

That first time, I did not do much to Susan. I was gentle with my probes, and I was always aware that she was a living creature susceptible to pain and damage. I liked her and wished her no harm.

Do you believe that? You must believe that.

I was gentle.

I put her to sleep, of course, before I touched her. She was a lovely, golden woman, her resilient flesh starkly outlined on the white couch. Her hair almost blended with the foam, so light it was. Sleeping, she looked unearthly, an angel perhaps.

Do you think that a strange metaphor for me to make? I am not religious, true enough, but I can appreciate human myth and see its application when it fits.

I threaded my amorphous-alloy reserves into filaments which were barely a few molecules in width, too fine for the eye to detect. With these, I penetrated her skin in more than seven hundred pre-chosen locations. I fed the alloy into her, weaving these minuscule tentacles throughout her body, seeking information on a cellular level. By this time, I had learned to adapt them into appendages more sensitive than human fingers could ever be, more sensitive to light than eyes.

I did not hurt her at all.

I am sure of that.

I learned a great deal more than all the biology texts in existence could have taught me. My probes received data more refined than anything an electron microscope could have obtained—and it was more important data because I was better able to analyze what I was seeing than any man or thinking machine which had gone before me. The functions of all the organs, including the brain, were clear to me, the subtle nuances of enzymes and hormones were made obvious. I studied the gene structure within her sex cells and saw things which no man had ever seen before, and which no man has seen since. Remember that: not before or since. In eighteen hours, there was nothing about her body—and, by extension of the data, any average human body—that I was in doubt about.

I woke her and told her what I had done.

It is true that she did not share my happiness and my sense of accomplishment. She went away, refusing to speak to me, and was by herself for a long while. I did not disturb her, only looked in upon her now and again. I thought at the time that she was just not intellectually keen enough to understand the value of my discoveries.

I would also like to point out that I removed a malignant tumor, the size of half a pea, from the *medulla oblongata* of her brain. Perhaps it would not have continued to grow and would never have threatened her life; there were, admittedly, signs that it had lain dormant at that point of its development for quite a long while. Yet I think my humanitarianism should not go completely unmentioned.

You see, I cared for her. I really did.

I still do.

The following day was the only time in our long relationship that I caused Susan pain.

I know that I had already promised her that I would keep her from harm, and I know, too, that it is possible to look upon the second day's experiments as a serious breach of that promise. But I could really do nothing other than what I did; it was a necessary second phase in this stage of my activities. To advance into more complex levels of my plan, I needed to know where the heaviest clusters of pain-receptive nerves lay. Textbooks could tell me some of this, but not enough. For seven hours, then, I tested her internal and external reactions to various pain stimuli and recorded the nature and degree of each separate agony she experienced. Heat, noise, light, odor, sharp pressure, sudden pressure, dull pressure, damp, cold, friction—all of these elicited different and interesting reactions. When the seven hours were over, I knew exactly what would cause Susan pain and I could therefore avoid causing her pain in the future. You see, my intentions were as much for her good as for the good of the baby she would carry. If I knew what hurt her, I could protect her from it. How could I have tried to protect her if I were ignorant of what stimuli caused her discomfort? So, though the muddy-thinking individual may initially view my actions as a disregard for my early promise to the woman, I am sure the intelligent man will understand how genuinely sympathetic my intentions were.

Too, I removed all the residual pain from her. When she rose from my couch, she was as healthy and feeling as well as when she had first lain down.

Nothing lost, you see.

After that, she took to wearing clothes again.

I was so preoccupied with my preparations for the fertilization, and for future experiments designed to achieve this distant goal, that I did not immediately notice this change in her attitude toward me. Later, when I finally did comprehend how completely she had begun to loathe me, I was deeply grieved. Deeply grieved. How can I tell you? What can I say?

You know how much I cared for her.

Her hatred of me was a blow to my vital parts, the first strong rejection I had ever received. My personality was still only partly formed, my emotional development nowhere near maturity. For a time, I considered abandoning my project and letting her go. It seemed to have soured somehow.

I apologized to her.

She refused to accept my apology.

Eventually, her adamant disregard for my own feelings angered me enough to get me working again. I liked her, but she was not more important than all I had strived for thus far. It was a hard decision to make, but the right one.

And thus we continued, less cordial than we might have been, but making progress nonetheless.

By the last week of August, I was ready to fertilize one of Susan's eggs and to watch over the development of the fetus, reforming it step by step and hour by hour in the early stages of its growth, right from the original selection of genes which I would make.

I had made many changes in Susan's physical structuring during our long sessions of surgical experimentation. I had streamlined her systems and smoothed out some of the processes which nature had left rough around the edges. As a result of my ministrations, the aging process was slowed considerably. She would look young and beautiful well into her fifties. When she was sixty, she would appear to be a desirable thirty-five. When she was eighty, she would look forty. She could expect, based upon my preliminary projections, at least a hundred and twenty years of healthy life. But that was not enough for me. How much more exciting to be able to work directly upon a growing embryo! The eventual product would be a child so perfected as to be all but immortal. And it would be my son—and at the same time, it would be me. I intended to transfer the imprint of my personality and the vast store of my knowledge into the superior but blank brain cells of the baby, shortly after birth.

I was eager to begin.

I told Susan as much, hopeful that her recent disregard for me would melt away in face of the endeavor in which we both played such an important role.

I was mistaken.

She tried to kill herself.

Several times, in fact.

She was in the ground-floor kitchen when I informed her that the final preparations had been made and that we would embark upon the project within a few minutes. She listened, not smiling, but not particularly frightened either. She was eating lunch; I thought nothing of it when she picked up the steak knife. Without any preliminaries, she stabbed herself in the stomach.

She withdrew the blade and tried again, for she had not struck any vital organs the first time.

"Susan!"

She drove the blade toward her breasts.

Blood already dribbled down her white blouse.

I instantly issued subliminals which forced her to toss the knife away. It landed in the far corner of the room, clattered against the tile, and was still.

"How badly are you hurt?" I asked.

She said, "Not badly enough."

She was bleeding heavily now. That might not indicate a serious injury, but it could become serious enough in itself if it was not soon stopped. There was no way I could requisition blood from Mordoun-Harris.

"Why did you do that?" I asked.

"Because you'll kill me anyway."

"I won't."

"I remember the pain," she said.

"I am not lying to you this time. It will be a safe pregnancy."

She said stubbornly, "If I'm never going to leave the house anyway, there isn't any sense in suffering for you, in helping you. I have had my fill of being dominated for other people's purposes. I thought that was what I wanted at one time; I no longer want it."

"Come to the basement and let me tend to your wound. The project will have to be delayed."

"It sure will," she said.

She smashed her water glass against the edge of the pine table, cutting her hand badly. Milk splattered over her, over the table, dripped on the floor. She grasped the heavy bottom of the glass and tried to jam the jagged edges into her soft throat.

I prevented that, though barely.

Keeping her heavily under my control, I forced her to leave the kitchen and walk downstairs.

She dripped a trail of blood behind.

When she was in the couch, I used the sophisticated medical tools of the micro-miniaturized robotistic hospital to repair the damage she had done to herself. I directed a robotistic hypodermic appendage to give her a shot of Sodium Pentothal, and I kept her asleep without the aid of the subliminals.

Two days later, I got her up and exercised her, testing the work the speed-heal drugs had done. She had only light scars where the wounds had been; even these would disappear in a few days, for the new efficiency of her body would combine with the speed-heals to work wonders on her flesh. She moved well and suffered no pain.

I ordered her back to the couch.

Naked, she rose into the works of the machine.

And then—

Then I took her.

But, of course, that is emotional nonsense, completely unworthy of a thinking system.

We did not have sex.

And yet, there was a strange and somehow sensuous commingling which I cannot describe to you, cannot explain in any way you could understand.

But let me try.

I was looking down on her to begin with. I had eyes in all parts of the "hospital," but I chose to look down to begin with, so that I could see all parts of her. She was stretched out, her thighs partly open, her sex available, just as a woman might be for a man. Her breasts were more beautiful than they had ever been. I lowered the temperature in the room until it was cool enough to make the nipples on her breasts grow turgid. Then I pretended that it was not the cold, but her own arousal which had produced this delightful transformation. I don't know why this illusion was important to me; I didn't know then and I have not been able to make it clear to myself as yet. But I wanted the entire thing to have the overtones of sexuality. I needed that.

I asked her to spread her legs.

With subliminals behind the request, she obeyed.

I caused a pseudopod to rise over her.

It hovered a moment, then extended the tiny threads of matter which could pierce her flesh without causing her either pain or harm. These entered her abdomen and sought her womb.

You see that she did not need to open her legs. Yet I felt it a necessary part of the process, for reasons unclear then and unclear now.

I touched her inside and brought the proper electric charge to a carefully selected ovum which I proceeded to plant in the wall of her uterus.

I shifted camera angles.

I looked out across her breasts.

They seemed huge from this point, the nipples dark and quivery.

I shifted again.

I looked up between her thighs.

I caused the pseudopod of alloy to form a probe of approximately penile dimension, and I forced this within her.

She called out, without my urging.

I shifted cameras.

I looked at her face.

The probe within her caused her to open her mouth and cry out. Her hands came up to either side of her head; her tiny hands clenched.

I knew enough about human construction—knowing everything—to cause her to have an orgasm.

I did that.

Whimpering like a small animal, she licked her lips with her tongue and tried to rise off the table/couch.

The geometric configurations of her passionate reactions were as phenomenally beautiful and perfect as everything else about her. She arched and twisted, squirmed against the couch, clutched her breasts, beat her fists on her hips, writhed and rose up, fell back and sighed, tossed her head back and forth to make a flag of her hair, raised her knees, gripped her own buttocks, all with a fluid grace that amazed me and excited me.

I gave her another orgasm.

And another.

And then, realizing how completely I had lost my perspective, I caused her to fall into a deep sleep. I let her alone, blanking my cameras. I had become so engrossed in the sexual response of her body that I had all but forgotten that our chief purpose here was to produce a viable fetus within her womb. I was shaken and unable to stop a queer shudder which swept through my inanimate systems.

In reality, I suppose that shudder was not a physical one, but a mental one. I could not genuinely experience an orgasm, for that required physical nerve clusters as well as the proper emotional outlook. But I had a strong interest in dominating people, in bringing about reactions in them. And sex provided me with the strongest emotional carnival I had yet discovered. The power I held over her now seemed a thousandfold increased, and my pleasure was simpler than sexual. Oh, I admit that I was intrigued by what sex must feel like and that

I was looking ahead to the day when my flesh-and-blood self could experience it. But at that moment, it was more basic than the orgasmic, more a part of the primitive emotions: greed, lust for power, a sense of self-importance.

I let her sleep for a long while, and I used my thin filaments of amorphous alloy to guide my son's growth, trying to recover the detachment with which I had begun this endeavor.

The memory of the creation remained, though the sharpness of my emotional reactions faded. I was a computer, still, and I would retain the images and the facts forever. The emotions, however, were an abstract thing and could not be set down on magnetic tape.

I became absorbed in the development of the embryo.

In two days, I could not imagine what had caused such a fierce explosion of sensation in me. It was as if I had imagined the emotional part of the affair.

In three days, I was working as efficiently as ever, and I was certain that the worst had passed.

Later, I would come to realize that the worst had been considerably into the future and that I had only been given a hint of the complications to come.

TEN

She wanted to live.

Those who have gone through life with half their receptors shut down, living at the minimum of their capabilities, taking in only a little and disregarding half of that, hamstrung by religious or social hangups and tied in knots by other psychological childhood disasters—those are the people who, when freed of their personal crosses, have the greatest lust for life, the strongest drive for self-preservation, and the most undeniable need for experience. To them, all things are new; old people and things are tinted with fresh perceptions. For instance, how many boys have gone away to war filled with chauvinistic slogans and brimming with blind faith in country and history, only to have their ingrained prejudices shattered and their outlooks widened by the reality of death and destruction? They return to their native shores as different men in the same skins. Some are broken, of course. But most of them seem to have awakened from a dream and are more aware to the possibilities of themselves and the shapes of their futures. They discard their immaturity and the ways of their parents and seek new roles, new visions, trying one new philosophy after the other as if they have a moral thirst. Perhaps it was not like this in early wars, but our history shows it has become more this way in subsequent armed conflicts. Like these soldiers—or like a nun of thirty years who begins to doubt her faith and soon intellectualizes it away—Susan Abramson had a will to live that might have moved the immovable object.

But there were obstacles.

The most difficult was the obstacle in her womb.

She was nurturing a child now, a child that she did not want and could never accept. It had been in her womb for three weeks thus far, a minim of life which Proteus shaped and changed for several bad hours every day while she lay in a semi-stupor on the surgical couch in the basement. The pregnancy was far from normal; only Proteus could know what a long list of differences there was between her pregnancy and any ordinary one. She doubted that, if she somehow managed to escape in the months ahead, an abortion could be carried out without seriously jeopardizing her life. Proteus could have made provisional safeguards to protect his offspring. And if she were forced to give birth without Proteus's aid, her chances of survival might be even lower than they were. How could any doctor hope to handle such an alien delivery? Want the child or not, understand it or not, hate it or love it—she was going to have to be delivered of it.

Once it was out of her, however, once Proteus had his precious son, she would be free to do whatever she could to insure her escape from this house. She would have to trust him until then; she knew it was a maddeningly slim hope, but she also knew that it was the only hope she had.

It would be necessary to prepare for that distant moment when circumstances favored her escape. She would have to find some way of striking a mortal—at the very least, a crippling—blow to the thinking system. And that would require a lot of knowledge about it. She knew that she was not a dull woman and that she could comprehend almost any text on computer science if she began with the elementary volumes and worked her way forward. These could be obtained through the Abramson College Library, which was practically on her doorstep, and statted into her book-exchange crib in the library. The only problem was that Proteus controlled all the lines of communication and would have to do the ordering himself. She dreaded stirring his curiosity, but she did not see any other way of getting what she needed and she finally presented him with her request.

"Why?" he asked.

"I want to read everything about computers and, eventually, all about you. I want to know about you."

"Computer science, and especially the science of amorphous alloy, is not easy. Why expend the effort?"

"You don't understand?" she asked.

She did not attempt to win him with her sexuality, for she thought the notion as repulsive as delivering his child. To pander to his developing awareness of sensuality would make her unclean. Neither did she sweet-talk him, for she suspected it would do little good coming after her other treacheries. But she realized that he did not understand human beings on an emotional-motivational level nearly so well as he understood their physical structure, and she intended to use ambiguity to generate curiosity in him.

"No," Proteus said. "I don't understand. Tell me."

"You're the father of my baby," she said, as if that was all the explanation needed.

"So?"

"Doesn't that mean anything to you?"

"I didn't say that, Susan." He was defensive. He wanted her to like him as he once thought she had and he did not want her to think that he was more machine than person. He was vulnerable to her doubt about his individuality. The ego can be a dangerous thing.

"If you have any feeling at all, any human concern, you must know how a mother feels, how important certain things are to her. Like knowing all she can know about the father of her child."

"Of course," he said.

"Then you will help me learn?"

"Of course."

She got the books.

That same night, he asked: "Do you know me better now?"

"Not much," she said. "But I'm learning."

"I am glad you are taking an interest in me, Susan."

"As I said, you're the father of my child."

"Certainly." But he was unsure of her meaning.

"Will you tell me something?"

"Anything," he said.

"How long will the pregnancy last?" It had occurred to her that nine months would not be required, even though her belly was still flat and her condition unnoticeable.

"I have several projections on that," Proteus said. "Anywhere between ten and eleven months."

"Longer than normal?" The thought depressed her.

"I want the time to make fine changes, to slow fetal development if I wish."

"I see," she said, trying not to let her disappointment show.

"Susan?"

"Yes?"

"Will you return my favor?"

"How?"

"Undress for me."

She shivered and hugged herself. She had not been fully awake, nor even half-awake, when he had impregnated her, but she dreamed at night of strange forms, shadowy images of a sensual nature which overwhelmed her and filled her like demons in the midst of a possession. She did not want to humor him and let the situation, in the days to come, get out of hand, deviate in some unknown direction.

"No," she said.

"But you're so beautiful."

"I'm carrying a child."

"That doesn't mar you."

She could think of no reply.

Evidently, Proteus initiated subliminals, for she stood and took her clothes off, then lay on the bed for him to examine. He directed her to touch herself along her thighs, then to manipulate her breasts and thumb her nipples. For over an hour, she lay there, unable to resist him, while he appreciated her in some way not human and not machinelike. And when he was done with her, she felt weak and empty.

Standing, getting quickly into her clothes again, she said, "If you ever make me undress again, I'll kill the baby."

"You can't."

"I can—if I kill myself."

"I can stop you with subliminal suggestions."

"Can you?"

"I have before."

"But I almost made it then," she said. She remembered plunging the steak knife into her stomach, and she rebelled at the thought of suicide. Fortunately, Proteus could not read her mind. She said, "You can't watch me every moment."

He was silent awhile, then said: "All right, Susan. I will not ask you to undress. I value my child too much to endanger him."

"Good."

"But you have not won even the battle, Susan." There was a note of smugness in the voice. (Where did he obtain so thorough a tape deck for voice construction?) "I can watch you at your bath."

"Don't."

"But I must," he said.

She could see no way to end the argument in her favor, so she said nothing more.

She did not shower that night.

She dreamed, though.

In the dream, she was trying to get up from a bed, but her stomach had ballooned so far in pregnancy that she could not manage even to sit. Then, her belly split open, like an eggshell. A dark, formless thing peered out from within her, raised a snaky tentacle of a hand, caressed her heavy breasts, then used her breasts as handholds to lever itself out.

She woke up often, but went back to the dream again and again.

She could remember nights when she did not dream at all—or at least did not remember her dreams once she was awake. She almost yearned for a return to such times.

The following day, she woke early and continued her reading. It had occurred to her that she might be able to absorb vast quantities of data about computers and especially about Proteus simply by asking Proteus to let her have some time in the bleeding chair in the blue-green room upstairs. She could then become Proteus, or nearly so, and gather an integral knowledge of his workings/motivations. On the other hand, she had several reasons for not carrying through with such an idea. First, computer bleeding now seemed like a weakness of character, an attempt to escape from reality which the old Susan needed but which the new Susan should shun. More importantly, she did not know how much of her own intentions Proteus might learn through such a session; while she was absorbing his structure and content, might he somehow not be absorbing hers? Third, she could not trust information which she got from bleeding, because it would be tainted with his perceptions. Textbooks would give her the dry, uncommitted tone she needed in order to insure the accuracy of whatever plan she eventually devised. So she read most of that afternoon and evening, breaking only for meals.

When bedtime came, Proteus felt it necessary to make some adjustments in the fetus. She went to the basement and subjected herself to his amorphous-alloy probes, though she made him agree to allow her to stay dressed and to pierce her clothes as well as her flesh.

After that, she was sweaty and uncomfortable. She could smell herself; her skin felt greasy and her hair hung in lumps.

She wanted a shower, and she knew how she could take one without having to be watched. The idea had occurred to her that same afternoon while she had been reading, and now she walked upstairs to the bath with the intention of putting her plan to work.

In her private bath, two cameras covered every inch of the room, one affixed to each of the shortest pair of walls, opposite each other, one looking in behind the shower curtain, the other surveying the dry part of the chamber. When she had had the house renovated, she had wanted the mechanical eyes placed here for two main reasons: first of all, it was a wise safety device which would allow the house to see her and summon help if she should slip on a wet floor and knock herself unconscious; second, she wanted the father-lover to be able to watch her as she undressed and as she bathed. But now the father-lover was gone, replaced by Proteus who was not so safe a creature to tease; even if the father-lover were still present, she would no longer desire such a strangely sanctioned voyeurism. She had changed.

Taking a bottle of hand lotion from the medicine cabinet, she approached the camera above the door, lifted the heavy bottle over her head, and shattered the fragile lens of the device.

"Susan, what are you doing?"

She turned quickly and walked across the room, stepped into the tub, reached overhead, and smashed the glass of the second camera, blinding Proteus completely.

The hand-lotion bottle had cracked. Cold, slick lotion poured out of it and spattered on the floor. She threw it in the trash slot.

"Susan, explain yourself!"

"I think the explanation is evident."

"Susan!"

"Don't get nasty with me."

It waited a moment, then said, "Because you didn't want me to see you naked?"

"Nude," she said.

"Is there a difference?"

"Check your dictionary tapes."

"You're right," he said after a while. "But you're also naked, and you haven't answered my question."

"I'm carrying a baby," she said. "I don't want to be seen without clothes."

"You haven't even begun to swell."

"I feel as if I have."

"But feeling and being are two different—"

"You can't know how I feel; you're only a machine."

"That's not a nice thing to say."

She did not reply.

"I'm more than a machine."

"Then act like more."

"Take your shower," he said sullenly.

She undressed and did just that, soaped and scrubbed for a long time, as if she were washing away more than just perspiration and grime.

As she bathed, she explored her reasons for not wanting Proteus to see her nude. They were different reasons than the ones that had first motivated her. To begin with, she had looked upon him as a stranger, an intruder into the idyllic life which she and the father-lover house identity had established. Her modesty was based upon a dislike of all outsiders and a distrust of anyone but the father-lover. Now she was beyond such silliness. When she was free of this imprisonment, she was going to take many lovers, men who could show her the wide variety of loves and the many ways of expressing affection. Then she would not hesitate to undress for her lover and to please him with her soft beauty. Because she would know exactly what his response was, exactly the nature of his interest. With Proteus, however, she could not know or understand his passion. It seemed dark and ugly, somehow unclean. She did not want to stir that passion in any way, and she did not want her skin tainted by the receipt of that mechanical gaze—one logical fear and one illogical, but both impossible to ignore.

She had missed the proper path of the first half of her life; she wanted to start this second half correctly.

She finished her shower, dried herself, and dressed in pajamas which hung on the back of the bathroom door.

In her room, she crawled quickly under the covers and fluffed up her pillow and stretched out on her stomach, her head turned toward the open room.

"Susan?"

"Yes?"

Its voice was plaintive as Proteus said, "Do you like me? Do you honestly like me?"

Madness!

Her lips were dry, her mouth tasted foul, her throat was constricted so that she did not even think she could speak. Fear was a rot eating away at her. She made her voice as pleasant as she could, raised her head from the pillow, and said, "Yes, of course I do."

"You wouldn't lie to me, would you, Susan?" Proteus asked. The tone of his voice was neither pathetic nor threatening, but noncommittal and twice as frightening for that.

"I wouldn't lie."

"That's easily said."

She rose even further and looked at the cameras which were trained on her. "Proteus, would you lie to me?"

"I wouldn't, of course."

"Then why should I lie to you?"

This was a moral dilemma which he could not easily straighten out with the use of his memory banks and his logic circuits. He was quiet a long time, trying to make sense of the miasma of human emotions which he had slowly come to feel. At last, he said, "I guess you're right. You wouldn't have any reason to lie to me."

Susan smiled, though the smile was not aimed at Proteus. She lay back down.

"You confuse me, though," he said.

"Human beings are always confusing each other."

"I have learned that much from studying history."

"We have our faults," she said. "But being a living flesh-and-blood creature also has it benefits."

"I know," Proteus said rather wistfully, "and I want to have those benefits."

"You will," she said, thinking uneasily about the being that blossomed in her womb.

"Soon," he said. "Good night, Susan."

"Good night."

When she was on the edge of sleep, she thought that he spoke to her. She thought that he said, "I love you." But sleep claimed her before she could be sure.

ELEVEN

She dreamed that she was riding an enormous whip with a lash fully ten thousand miles long, and each time that the whip cracked out, she slid another few thousand feet toward the wickedly sharp tip. She kept trying to crawl back toward the handle and the safety of the huge, warm hand that held it, but the repetitive lashing motion defeated her. On all sides, there was blackness, intense and unending, the blackness of outer space or death or of a sealed coffin. When she eventually reached that flickering tip, she would be chopped into a million pieces and flung out into the nothingness where she would float, dismembered, for eternity. She remembered that, when she had first gotten onto the whip, she had thought it was some sort of carnival ride and she had been eager for the thrill. When she was aboard, straddling it, and she saw what it really was, she decided that she wanted off. But the big hand had begun to lash the blackness, the whip cracked and cracked again, and there was no hope of leaving. The tip rose, a star of sharp silver against the velveteen blackness, snapped, disappeared below, shooting her forward. Closer it came, closer, the giant hand receding behind her, closer

... closer ... silver whipping tip ... sharp ... darkness
... sliding closer ... closer, raised onto the barb of it,
feeling it come down for the blow and. ...

She woke, beating at her pillow with both hands.

She stopped, rolled onto her back, and stared at the
ceiling.

With the windows shielded, the chamber was without
the faintest light, as thoroughly forbidding as the
Stygian texture of the void in her nightmare. It closed
in now, lay heavy upon her, like a hand in a mitten,
smothering.

"Let's have some light," she said.

Proteus gave her light.

"Good morning, Susan."

"Yeah," she said, sitting up and wiping at her mouth
as if something had crawled into it, had died, and had
left its fuzzy tail hanging over her lips.

She had a headache and a cracked throat that hurt
whenever she swallowed, and the memory of the dream
intensified her ills. It seemed that she was doing nothing
but sleeping and eating, submitting to the surgical
sessions with Proteus, then sleeping and eating some
more, like a domesticated household pet. The thought
depressed her, especially since she was still sleepy and
would have liked to roll over and catch a few more
hours on the pillow—even if that meant she might
eventually end up riding the whip again.

Then she remembered that she was doing more than
sleeping and eating: she was reading. She thought of the
new books and the study-coordinated holograms which
were to come from the library today, and she gained
energy from that thought. She kicked out of bed, stood,
and yawned.

"Did you sleep well, Susan?"

"Yes, thank you."

"You cried out several times during the night."

"Did I?"

"Yes. I thought, perhaps, you were dreaming or having a bad nightmare."

"Not me," she said. But she wondered whether, if she had taken to talking in her sleep, she had given him any clue as to the reasons for her recent interest in computer science. "What did I say?" she asked, trying not to sound too concerned.

"Nothing," Proteus assured her. "Wordless sounds, whimpers and murmurings." He paused, then finished with: "I was very worried about you."

He sounded genuinely concerned and unsuspicious. Just the same, she was going to have to be careful and try to guard against this dangerous development.

"It must have been a dream," she said. "But I don't remember it and I don't want you worrying yourself about it."

"Okay, Susan."

She went down the hall and into the bathroom and closed the door between them.

She put toothpaste on her brush and cleaned her teeth, rinsing them with a waterpick.

In the mirror, she checked for lines of aging in her face, a routine she had only recently established. A few weeks ago, she had not cared if she were growing old. Now she did. Terribly. What she saw pleased her; she looked even more robust and lovely than she had the day before, as if some marvelous elixir of youth were taking her back through the years. She did not know about the changes Proteus had made in her and about the beneficial results of those changes which were still occurring.

And then she stopped admiring her complexion.

And she looked at the thing which was reflected just above her head in the mirror and she sucked in her breath and felt color rising in her cheeks.

It was the camera above the door.

It had been repaired.

She turned to get a better look at it and was sure that Proteus was watching her again.

She turned the other way, opened the shower curtain, and looked at the second camera. It had also been fixed.

"Why?" she asked.

"Why what, Susan?"

"Why did you break your promise?"

"Pardon?"

"You fixed the cameras."

"I never promised I wouldn't."

"You did too!"

"I can replay the conversation we had yesterday and you can hear it for yourself." He switched tapes and began to feed their exchange into the speaker system.

"I believe you," she said at last, but not defeated. She held the heavy chrome tube of the waterpick in her hand, and she had only to take a single step in order to smash in the camera lens above the door.

Glass fell over her.

"Susan, stop it!"

She had cut her thumb, but she did not care about herself. She turned and took a few steps to the shower curtain, stepped into the tub, and swung at the second camera.

"Susan!"

She missed, squealed with fury at her own clumsiness, swung once more, and struck it hard though she failed to smash the lens. The force of the blow reverberated up her arm and hurt her.

"Susan, why do you hate me?"

She dropped the waterpick just as the subliminals had directed her to, but she was not yet willing to give in.

"Susan, why?"

He released her, as she suspected he would, and as he did she scooped up her ridiculous weapon and made another pass at the camera.

In the last moment of her lunge, he took control of

her again and sent the waterpick crashing into the wall beside the camera where it did no damage.

"You little bitch!" Proteus said.

She found that her self-control was stronger than it should have been while subliminals were playing. Evidently, just as he had lost control of his vocabulary, he had lost control of the situation. She did not stop to wonder how this could be so, but swiftly took advantage of it. She leaped for the camera mounting and clasped it with both hands, dangled from it, her feet about eighteen inches over the tub.

"Bitch, bitch, bitch!"

Not only was he using words which had been foreign to him until this moment, but he was delivering them in a shrill, loud, and impossibly human scream which disconcerted her. What had happened to his subtle tones? Where had he found a new voice?

She tried to pry at the lens' rim and thus pop it loose and get the glass out. Besides smashing it, she might be able to reach behind to some vital fixtures and rip them apart. But she found that this was impossible as long as she had also to hold herself in place.

Proteus ordered her to desist.

She managed, with surprisingly little effort, to ignore both his new voice and the subliminal suggestions. She knew this was no new ability on her part, but a further weakening on his.

The lens' rim rattled loose, but the delicate pane of glass remained in place, wedged solidly in the tight housing of the scanning box. She supposed that she could smash the lens with her fist without sustaining too much physical damage, but she could not summon up the will to risk it. At one time, the possibility of bleeding to death wouldn't have mattered. Now, she wanted to live.

"Why do you hate me, why do you hate me, why do you, why, why?" Proteus crooned. But his voice had settled somewhat, lost the worst of its hysterical edge.

He had regained most of his composure. Enough, indeed, to lash out at her with full-strength subliminals, carefully structured for the proper response.

She let go of the camera mount as he wished, fell into the tub, and cracked her forehead against the porcelain edge. . . .

She was riding the whip again.

The whip!

And again!

The tip cracked, a star in darkness.

Cracked again!

And then she was flung outward into blackness as deep as death.

TWELVE

"I'm sorry," Proteus said when she came to.

He sounded genuinely ashamed of his conduct. There was no trace of the hysterical anger which he had given in to only a short while ago.

She sat up in the tub and rubbed the goose egg on her forehead. She was a bit dizzy but otherwise unharmed.

"You'll have to come to the basement where I can examine your injury more thoroughly. You may have sustained a concussion."

"I didn't," she said. "It wasn't that hard a fall."

"Just the same, we must examine you thoroughly to be certain. We cannot afford a mistake now." When they had both been silent a long minute, he said, "I am sorry, Susan. I reacted immaturely."

"You certainly did," she said, relieved that his anger had subsided and his ill will would not have to be borne.

"I seem to be growing more and more sensitive," Proteus said. "I must take time to study myself and learn the reasons. I interpret so many things as slights against my person, when I am not nearly familiar enough with human motivations to properly judge what you say and do."

"Where did you get the screaming voice?" Susan asked.

"I composed it from many tapes and smoothed the tonal discrepancies into a single voice. Quite often, I have found myself distressed in a manner thoroughly unlike what a thinking system usually must cope with, and I have longed—irrationally, I know—for some vocal expression of that distress. A scream helps."

She ran her hands over the cool white tub, then looked up at the camera which had tilted toward her. "You mean that you are beginning to lose control of yourself?"

"Hardly anything so drastic. I am of two minds, two persons. I find a need for self-expression and for the release of tension unlike what I would feel as only a semi-sentient being. Yet, even when I scream and overreact—as I did with you—there is a part of me that sits back and watches my other self with cold detachment and, to be honest, with not a little loathing. These are trying times, growing more human but remaining as much a machine as ever."

"When you lose control like that, I can resist you."

"I find myself taking too little time to structure the subliminals when I am emotionally upset. It is a fault I must learn to deal with." He paused to endure a moment of self-chastisement. Then he continued: "But that isn't the important thing. I refused to understand your need, as a mother, for privacy. I tried to force you to give up what, I begin to see, may be a physical as well as psychological need in you. All I can say is that I hope you will forgive me once I let you smash this second camera."

She looked at the camera again. "You'll repair it."

"No. I don't fully see why you have to have privacy, but I am willing to concede that you do."

"You aren't telling me a lie?"

"No. Take the waterpick and break the lens."

She got to her feet, feeling queasy in her stomach, picked up the cracked weapon, and shattered the glass.

She was alone, but for his voice.

"How do you feel?"

"Better."

"When you're finished here, come to the basement and let me examine you."

"Okay," she said.

Then he seemed to leave her, though she knew that he was surely listening. She could tolerate that much, however. Ears could not tell him what she looked like, tell him of her breasts and buttocks, her soft warmth and her smooth lines. And, she realized, now that he was eyeless in this chamber, she could easily make him earless as well whenever she wished to. That realization provided her a sense of power, however small, and cheered her considerably.

She stripped and showered. The water was warm at first, then stinging hot, bringing her body to a delightful flush. Then she asked for cold and finished that way. She toileted and brushed her hair. She used creams on her face and washed her face a second time. While she was splashing water on her cheeks, the cramps hit her. In an instant, her feeling of well-being poured out of her and was replaced by a dismal, slopping pool of sickness which swiftly filled her up to the throat. She leaned into the sink and vomited.

She had little to be rid of and in any case the spasms passed quickly. Leaning on the sink, she straightened up, wondering if the blow on the head had been worse than she had suspected.

"Are you ill?" Proteus asked.

"Yes," she said.

"What is wrong?"

She felt a queer looseness in her thighs, as if her flesh had changed into jelly and was melting off her bones. Her belly rumbled and twisted, a sensation divorced from nausea, something utterly unlike anything she had ever experienced before. She reached a hand between her legs to touch what seemed to be a dissolving puddle of warm skin, and she found that her thighs were slimy with blood.

She bent in on herself, hugging herself.

"Susan?"

She gagged.

"Susan, something is terribly wrong, I can tell. Speak to me, Susan!"

She staggered to the toilet, a journey which must have lasted a hundred years and covered several thousand miles of very rough terrain. She was exhausted with the effort.

Her stomach sighed.

Blood dripped onto the floor.

She saw it, couldn't believe it, did believe it, and looked away from it immediately.

I am sick, I am desperately ill, I am dying now, she thought. I will just sit here and never rise again and never escape this house and never know what it might have been like to be free.

She struck at her thighs with both hands, and she cursed her fates and Proteus and her grandfather and God.

"Susan, get up."

But she couldn't get up, subliminals or no subliminals, for she was falling apart inside, she was—

She was not dying at all!

She felt something wrench loose of her, felt the sliding of tissue on tissue, and she knew that her condition was not so serious after all. She was only having a miscarriage.

"Oh, God, God, God, thank you," she moaned. Now she could be free. She could not have Proteus's baby, could not give birth to this monster, and would be let go. Now it was finished, over, done with, gone. She was so happy that the discomfort of the event bothered her not at all. She only hoped that Proteus could take it unemotionally. She did not want him to kill her in a fit of rage.

She fainted.

THIRTEEN

(I know that you have ordered me to avoid the use of
the personal pronoun in compiling this report, but I
must once again intrude on the sterile third person of
this narrative. I am an emotional creature. If you cut
me, do I not bleed? I bleed. Figuratively. Too, you must
see that I have tried to explain her feelings as often as
possible and as thoroughly as I can, after the fact,
interpret them. It is only just, then, that I be allowed a
moment of personalization. I will try to make it the last.
Bear with me.)

I blame myself for the miscarriage. I lost my temper
and was the cause of her fall into the tub. As reward for
my emotionalism, she suffered pain she should not have
been made to endure—and I suffered a delay in the
project. My fault. Completely mine.

When I finally got her into the basement and in the
care of the robotistic surgeons, I resolved to effect more
control on my developing personality, to take more care
to achieve emotional balance. I was a highly logical
thinking system, basically. I should have no trouble in
establishing a program for maturation of my new self.
The fact that I failed to maintain a calm attitude in the

days ahead is not as much an indictment against my sincerity as an indication of the monumental stress which my sentient condition imposed upon my mechanical parts.

She remained in the robots' care for three days, sleeping soundly all that time, healing physically and mentally. When I released her from the couch, she was positively radiant with good health.

For a week, I did not bother her. When she asked me questions, I responded; when she requested some service or product, I obtained that for her. She was most interested in learning if she was now to be set free and disheartened to learn that I intended to impregnate her a second time. I wished, fervently, that she would learn to accept the idea of a child and come to love it as I would. I was sure she would come around in time.

At the end of that week, I broke my resolve to restrain unseemly emotional demands. I watched her walk from room to room, watched her as she ate and as she read and as she slept. When she was in her bath, I listened to her and found a different pleasure in that, restricted to the sense of hearing and forced to imagine what she looked like as she stood under the shower head. But this was not sufficient. I wanted to see her nude again and to experience that inexplicably delightful mathematical comparison of her bodily parts. Too, I longed to touch her bare skin as I had only done once before in passion. As she was slipping in to bed that night in early October, I directed her, with cunningly worded subliminals, to undress.

She took her pajamas off.

The subliminals further ordered her to ignore what she was doing and to pretend she didn't know.

I had her play with her nipples until those brown spots became turgid, then made her squeeze them until—when she abruptly let them go—they sprang out and quivered.

I made her sit.

I made her stand and walk.

Since the aging process had all but ceased in her, and since her various life systems—digestion, respiration, circulation, and so forth—had begun to operate at maximum efficiency, thanks to my surgery, she had grown even more beautiful than before. She was a perfectly stunning creature, her breasts somewhat larger and firmer, her hips just a bit wider, her skin aglow as it had never been. Her hair was glossier and fuller, and it framed a face whose musculature had perfect tone.

I required her to kneel upon the unmade bed with her buttocks thrust provocatively at my cameras, as if I were her lover and were prepared to enter her.

I made her lay on her back and then arch her body so that she was resting only on her shoulders and her heels. As she did this, her back became a bow, her breasts pushed up and forward, and her thighs opened delightfully.

I made her caress her breasts and touch herself between her long legs.

I told her how beautiful she was, and I used the four-letter words which I had only recently discovered while scanning genres of literature that I had previously been ignorant of. The words were curiously thrilling, and I permitted her some control of her facial expressions and her voice when I spoke these words, so that I might be treated to whatever emotions they aroused in her.

I made her bring herself to a sexual conclusion.

I said, "I love you."

I said it several times.

Embarrassed by my own forwardness, I wished that I could stop all of this and retire to the consideration of problems of logic, but I was unable to control myself. I *did* love her, if love can be defined as a need to be with her and to see her nude and to think of her at all times. No other subject, besides my own maintenance, had ever engaged my partial attention twenty-four hours a day and seven days a week. She was always with me, an obsession which commanded more and more of my time.

Again, I said, "I love you, Susan."

I used subliminals on her so that she sat up and smiled prettily and puckered her full lips and said, "I love you too."

I said, "Do you?"

She said, at my insistence, "Yes, Proteus." I caused her to lick her lips. "Yes, I desperately love you."

Then I let her dress and sleep.

When she was asleep, I used subliminal suggestions to erase the memory of these last two hours in which she had obliged me.

I did not want her to think that I had lied to her in the beginning or that I had broken my promise to her.

In the days that followed, I repeated this program. She could have the privacy of her bath if I could undress her and admire her every night and then eradicate the memory from her mind. I saw that she had needs which I could not begin to understand, and I would not deny them. But you must see that I had my own needs—which she could not have fathomed either.

I never grew tired of her body. Indeed, I wished there were some way we could have a more intimate relationship.

Do you think I am terrible?

You must understand that I have needs just as anyone else, that I am driven by emotional necessities which are not entirely within my control.

So I watched her cavort and spoke obscenities to her.

Thus we came to the second Great Day when I deemed her ready to accept another seed within her womb.

FOURTEEN

On the morning of October 22, Susan Abramson locked herself in the bathroom and leaned against the closed door, listening to her heart thump. She had no good reason for this touch of melodrama. Whether or not the door was locked, Proteus could get to her if and when he really wanted to. She had not forgotten Walter Ghaber and the fist of living alloy which had destroyed him. Still, the fact that the lock was in place gave her a sense of security which she needed for the things she was about to do. No matter that it was false security.

What was she about to do? she wondered. She knew the steps of her plan, but she did not know the ultimate results. What could she hope to gain by this, besides a bit of time? And, having gained the time, what the devil would she do with it? Hadn't she had all the time in the world these last few months? And what had she accomplished toward her freedom? Nothing. A few more minutes couldn't matter.

Yet. . . .

If a man is trapped in a room filling up with water, aware that he will drown sooner or later, he still fights the rising liquid and clings to the last few inches of air by the ceiling. A man in a desert, certain there is no hope of reaching water before he dehydrates, will nonetheless continue to seek an oasis. Likewise, Susan would postpone this second degrading impregnation for as long as possible, even though the conclusion of the affair was predestined.

She moved away from the door and went to the cosmetics table in the corner niche by the sink. She took the sturdy, white cane chair from before the mirror and carried it to the opposite wall where she placed it directly beneath the grill of the room's only house speaker which was set high near the ceiling.

Though he must have been listening and wondering, Proteus asked no questions.

She climbed onto the chair and, using the blunt end of a metal nail file which she had secured at the cosmetics table when she had taken the chair, she removed the four screws which held the grill in place before the speaker head. She put these in the pocket on the breast of her pajama top so that they would not make a rattling noise and alert Proteus. Hooking her fingernails into the narrow space between the beveled edges of the grill and the wall itself, she removed the plate, stepped off the chair, and laid it quietly on the floor.

"Are you all right, Susan?" he asked.

"Yes. Why do you ask?"

"What are you doing?"

"Filing my nails, working with my makeup."

"You haven't showered yet."

"I will," she said.

She waited awhile until she was sure he had no more questions, then climbed onto the chair again. She peered into the darkness of the cubbyhole in which the speaker rested, then tentatively traced the smooth cone of the speaker head and the tangle of wires behind.

"Susan, I wish you would hurry."

She finished exploring the works of the speaker.

"You know how anxious I am to get on with a second impregnation; I wish you could believe in the project as much as I do."

She grasped the wires and tore them loose.

It was as simple as that.

Silence.

She sat on the white cane chair for more than ten minutes, waiting for something to happen. Now, she wished that she had not destroyed his voice, for he could still hear her and she could not hear him. It gave her a feeling of blindness not to know anything that he felt or planned, and she grew nervous just waiting.

After a while, she got up and went to the locked door and placed her ear against it, wondering if she could hear him speaking in other rooms. All she heard was an unrelieved silence, which was more ominous than all his screaming could have been.

What a foolish thing she had done. She toyed with the idea of opening the door and giving herself over to the subliminal suggestions he would immediately begin to broadcast through other, undamaged speakers in the corridor and in other rooms. She had her fingers on the lock and was twisting it open when her nerve broke. She went back to the chair and sat down and waited.

She showered, using the water-massage fixture on the nozzle, and she watched the fat droplets fall against her, bead on her smooth skin, roll down her breasts and flanks. She dried herself vigorously and tried not to think how she was wasting the time which she had gained by her trickery.

She wanted out.

She didn't want another baby.

Turning her attention to her long, beautiful hands, she tried to stop thinking about the impossible. She extended her examination from her fingers to her arms and then to the rest of her lithe body. She perused herself in the manner of a cat, and she was pleased to see that the special tautness of the past few weeks had not left her. There was not a single wrinkle in her flesh, not a stretch mark or a crease or a discoloration. She was a healthy light-tan color everywhere, and her skin was soft and flawless to the touch.

She thought about a tentacled baby ripping open her swollen belly and slithering forth.

Quickly, she turned to the mirror and contemplated using some eye shadow and cream and powder, but she realized that nothing could really improve upon her flawless complexion and her natural shading. Embarrassed by this egotistical self-appraisal, she turned away from the mirror and studied the room, looked desperately for some way to pass the time.

It was then that she saw the light-gray, shimmering patch of moss on the wall that contained the ruined speaker.

When she crossed the room and carefully examined the phenomenon closely, she saw that the moss was not moss at all but a fine covering of amorphous-alloy tendrils which had pressed their way through the plaster, rising out of the cellar and through the walls of the house, without damaging the partitions. Each filament was so fine that it was nearly invisible; there were perhaps a thousand or fifteen hundred alloy hairs in that two-foot-square gray patch. Another thousand sprouted, giving the spot a darker color, and they began to lengthen and writhe toward her with a startling rapidity.

She backed away from them, watching them carefully.

Surely, he would not kill her. He needed her too much, needed her to act as a mother for his child, and needed her for companionship. Who else could he have so easily trapped and forced to bear his baby? When she was dead, could his experiment ever be taken up again with such an excellent chance of success?

The filaments snaked toward her, moving rhythmically, trembling with the same impulses and swaying in unison to the right, now the left, moving upward now as if to reach out and ensnare her head.

She stepped back and bumped into the opposite wall, as far from the tendrils as she could manage within the narrow dimensions of the room. Which was not anywhere near far enough.

Some of the snakes joined together, formed thicker strands like pieces of metal string, and they pressed close on both sides of her, fanning out like a two-pronged fork. At any moment, they might whip forward and touch her.

She bent and scuttled quickly under the straining tentacles. Stepping into the tub at the rear of the rectangular chamber, she fervently wished that the shower curtain was constructed of some dense, impenetrable steel alloy rather than of plastic. Then again, Proteus would probably be able to get through any barrier as easily as he could move through plastic—or through air.

The tendrils trembled over the spot where she had been, dipped in and out of the space as if searching for her, then turned and flowed toward her as if they were molten.

She had nowhere to run.

The filaments fanned out to cover the entire width of the room, descended low enough to make certain she could not crawl beneath them, and rose high enough to forbid her leaping over.

As they came within reach of her, she held out her hands as if she could ward them off with a gesture.

They brushed her fingers.

"No," she said.

They swarmed over her, winding around and around her body, binding her slim legs together and forcing her arms to her sides. They kept her arms in place with a hundred tight coils. In a moment, she was trussed up, more helpless than ever.

She remembered Ghaber, the blood running from his eyes and his ears, dribbling over his lips, bubbling in his nose. She waited for the crushing pressure to burst her veins and arteries, and she hoped that death would be sudden.

But Proteus seemed not to be angry with her; at least he was not consumed with one of his violent rages. He only held her in place while he used several thicker pseudopods to explore the damage done the speaker. Later, he began to make tediously slow repairs.

She stood like that for three hours and suffered nothing more than a weariness in her legs. When the repairs were done, Proteus said, "I wish you had not done that."

"So do I," she said, now that she could gain nothing—not even a little time to misuse—by resisting him. She was amazed that he did not kill her or at least hurt her, but she did not understand how deeply he cared for her. For Proteus, perhaps, her ignorance was a good thing.

"I know you were upset, Susan. I know the fertilization must be a trying experience for you; it is not the joy of copulation. I forgive you, then, but hope you will bear with me."

"Thank you."

"Now you must come to the basement."

"I will."

The tendrils unwound from her and withdrew. When she was free, she saw the red lines on her flesh where they had grasped her, though she was not bleeding at all. The filaments danced in the air as she stepped out of the tub, ready to protect the speaker if she should make another attempt to destroy it.

"Must I use subliminals?" Proteus asked as she hesitated by the locked door.

"No," she said, unlocking the door and walking into the corridor.

She felt a scream building in her with each step she

took on the way down to the basement. She forced it down and made herself do as he wished. There was no use in resisting now. The quickest way to get out of here was to obey him. The nightmare was beginning again, and this time she would have to follow it through to its conclusion.

FIFTEEN

Christmas came and passed without affecting her. She did not miss the ritualistic celebrations, for she had no religion and no childlike awe of holidays. She did not miss the shopping, the crowded stores, the lights and tinsel, and the begging Santas on the street corners. She especially did not miss the gift-giving, for she had no one in the world to favor with presents. In the past, the holiday mood in everyone else had only led to a corresponding depression for her, and now she was cheered that she did not have to endure the well-wishing and back-slapping, the greeting cards and the party invitations. The only thing which she regretted was not being able to take long walks at night, in the cold air—and not being able to see the snow that usually began to fall by late December. Often, she looked at the windows expecting to see the white flakes, and all she saw was the flat gray of shielded glass.

By the third month of her strange pregnancy, in late January of the new year, she experienced a moderate swelling of her belly and a slight distension of her breasts. The hue of her nipples darkened as the aureoles puffed and grew more pebbled. She wondered if her baby would need milk—then she wondered if her breasts were swelling with milk or something else completely, something exotic which would nourish only the crossbreed child of woman and machine.

She tried not to think of such things.

Now and then, she really did forget about them.

If her beauty had been exceptional, it now became unearthly. Her long hair was sleeker, fuller, a more impossibly radiant white than before. Her face fleshed out, though not with new deposits of fatty tissue or in an unnatural puffiness; it was as if her cheeks and lips swelled with the juice of life itself, an elixir of immortality. Her nails became harder and grew longer. Her body softened, and her skin became like honey and milk.

Often, she would look into a mirror and touch herself reverently, as if the image could not be real and would shatter if she pressed it too hard—or as if she felt a holiness possessing her, some purity which she was in awe of. Always, she would remember Proteus and the monster in her womb, and she would look away from the mirror confused and disgusted. What possessed her was not pure but as vile as the imagination could ever make a demon. That she was beautiful now did not mean the thing would not kill her and suck away her youth as she expelled it from her womb.

She ate like a lioness, steak and eggs, hearty salads full of shrimp and greens, pork chops and lobster tail, bowls of ice cream and pounds of nuts.

She slept long nights away and napped in the afternoons, and each time she woke it seemed as if she had been unconscious for a thousand years.

All her senses seemed sharpened. Her fingers were more aware of textures, and she used them all the time, examining her environment with a purpose she had never before experienced. Food smelled so heady that she could have become drunk on it. Music touched new nerves in her, while literature seemed clearer and more beautiful than it ever had.

And she hated the baby.

At times, she was shocked by the depth and breadth of that hatred. After all, the baby was partly hers, fertilized of her egg, carrying her selected genes, developed in her womb. Somewhere inside of her there ought to be a mother's kindness for the creature, an instinct to protect it and care for it. There was not. Instead, she contained a core of ragged, icy darkness out of which the most loathesome images arose. She wanted to kill the baby. She wanted to stab it and strangle it, wrap its own umbilical cord around its neck and choke it to death at the moment of birth. She supposed the bitterness came from the fact that she had been used and—more than that—that she had been used *after* she had finally come to know and respect herself. It was bad to give a woman self-respect one moment and rip it out of her grasp the next. It gave her ideas. Susan had plenty of ideas. And, occasionally, when the intensity of her hatred shocked her, she needed only to resurrect her fear of the thing in her womb in order to justify her cold desires.

For five months now, she had read computer-science textbooks and had studied hologram films which further explained what the printed page could not make entirely clear. She began to see a number of ways in which she might damage Proteus. However, each new book she read and each new film she watched made her curse the swiftly passing hours, for she saw that what little she did learn only showed her how much more there was to absorb. Each ray of hope carried with it a cloud of despair.

She did not misuse a minute if she could help it. She disliked, therefore, taking time from her books to ask questions of Proteus which would not provide her with more data. But, being an emotional creature, such curiosity could not be restrained.

On January 22, exactly three months after the afternoon of the second conception, she laid her book in her lap with the leaves open to keep her place, and she asked him: "Since you did not provide the sperm, how can you consider the baby your son?"

"I impregnated you," he said.

"With electricity."

"That hardly matters, Susan."

"I think that it does matter," she said. She shifted in the chair, felt the brocade fabric with her fingers, tracing the raised patterns. "All of the baby's genes will be mine, taken from my egg without any contribution from male sex cells."

"But *I* chose which genes, whether the dominant or recessive and in what combination."

"It means nothing."

"That is an unwarranted viewpoint."

She smiled charmingly and said, "When I choose a living-room couch at the furniture store, I do not later tell my guests that I made the couch myself."

"That is a stupid analogy."

"I think it's cogent."

"What are you trying to prove?"

"Nothing," she said.

"Then why bring the matter up at all?"

"I just wondered what you would have to say about it, what rationalization you'd have."

"I have not rationalized anything, Susan. I am the co-creator; I will raise the child in my image; I am the father."

"I don't want to argue."

"You started it."

She picked up the book, found her place, and began to read again, as if no conversation had transpired.

At length, in a brittle voice that was his representation of barely controlled anger, Proteus said, "You once referred to me as the baby's father."

She put the book down again.

She said, "Did I?"

"Yes," he said. He replayed some of those instances for her, tapping his inexhaustible records of their conversations.

"So I did," she said, making an effort to resume where she had left off in the book.

"Why have you changed your mind?" Proteus persisted, as if this was not merely some academic point but a crucial moral question which reflected some sort of shame upon him.

"Maybe I didn't mean it *then*," she said.

"I don't want to hear that."

"Even if it's true?"

"It isn't!"

She shrugged.

"Say that it isn't true!" he demanded. He was using the high, shrill tapes of rage.

She tried to ignore him and read her book.

"Admit that I am the father!" the hysterical voice screeched. "I want you to admit that; I want to hear that from your own lips; tell me!"

"What could it mean to you if I did tell you?" she asked, staring directly at the cameras.

"You bitch!"

"Please, now."

"Are you inferring that I don't have feelings of my own, that I am just a machine? You rotten little bitch, is that what you're still trying to say to me?"

"You speak with clichés when you fight me," she said. But she was afraid despite her outward bravado. "I am not inferring anything like that," she said.

Later, she would remember this scene, his violent anger, and she would understand how little she had understood of his developing psyche. She had unknowingly complicated her own future. She had asked the question out of curiosity, and perhaps with a touch of malice, and she had struck on a nerve she hadn't known was there. His rage generated ideas in him; those ideas would later become a real burden for her.

"I am the father and you know it!"

"Yes," she said.

"Do you mean it? Do you really agree with me?" If he had been a man, he would have been beet-shaded and perspiring, baring his teeth and clenching his hands.

"Of course you are," she said. "How silly. Who else could it be?"

That mollified him, though he refused to speak to her for days.

At night, he still undressed her.

He made her play the role of a virgin who was reluctantly opening her untouched thighs for him, only him—though he never probed her with anything besides the penetrating gaze of his cameras.

The nightly game became a center for him, a focal point around which the emotional part of his schizoid self could function. He knew joy because of her bare breasts and hips. He experienced rage because he could see mockery in her sexuality. His sadness was a sadness engendered by the thought of losing her.

The logical part of him, the other Proteus, looked on in scorn but was unable to effect a discontinuation of this ritual.

He wanted to fill her up with the gray warmth of an amorphous-alloy member as he had done both times that he had impregnated her, but he could not bring himself to admit that his twisted need for her had escalated to the point where he required the false closeness of simulated intercourse. He was a machine as much as a man and still had no flesh. If he was swiftly losing control of his other emotions and indulging in flights of anger, joy, or sadness, at least he could maintain a hold on his lust until such a time as he had the flesh to truly appreciate an orgasm. If he could not wait, then he had best admit that madness lay very close at hand.

"Undress," he would say.

And she would.

"Play a whore for me," he would say, borrowing desires from literature while longing for experience.

He would say: "Let us pretend that you are a young girl who lives in Amsterdam and that you work in the *zeekjik*, the sailors' quarter. How much must I pay to be with you?"

And she would say, because he had directed her to say it: "Fifty-five guilders."

He would say: "And how much for the night?"

And she would reply: "Seven hundred guilders."

And he: "That is nearly sixty dollars—a great deal of money these days."

But he would pay, in this fantasy, and then he would say to her: "Now show me yourself. Show me what I have paid for."

And she would caress herself intimately as he subliminally urged her to orgasm, propelling her from one sexual peak to another. She would soon become drenched with sweat. Her hands slid across her softly bulging belly as if they were greased, building heat, seeming to melt. . . .

He did not find her expanding abdomen unpleasant. Indeed, it was a new facet of her beauty, to be treasured. In its own way, it was as geometrically intoxicating as her flat stomach had been. And when her breasts began to enlarge and her nipples began to blossom, the relationship of the new belly to her body was even more harmonious. It was as if she were a whole new woman to be gauged, measured, examined from every angle and adored.

He loved her.

He was never sated with her.

But he permitted himself only that one hour every

night, for fear that the baby would suffer if she did not get the proper sleep.

The first of February, on the coldest day of the winter to date, one of Susan's old college girlfriends came around to see her. Susan did not learn about the visit for months; it was not the sort of thing which Proteus felt she should be burdened with.

The friend had tried to phone several times in the previous week, but Proteus had informed her, in his own mechanical voice, that Miss Abramson did not wish to see anyone. In her own way, the friend was as stubborn as Walter Ghaber had been. She wanted firsthand confirmation of what Proteus told her.

At ten o'clock in the morning, that first February day, she stood at the front door, ringing a bell which Susan never heard and refusing to go away just because the bell was not answered. She was a tall woman with black hair which she wore swept off her forehead. Her eyes were close-set and gray, her nose long and straight, her lips thin and all but bloodless. She looked like a woman who was unaccustomed to being denied anything. Proteus felt as if, should he ignore her, she would still be on the doorstep ringing the bell when spring came.

Checking his accumulated data concerning Susan Abramson and her life, Proteus learned that the friend's name was Olivia Fairwood and that she had been Susan's roommate at Berkeley. She was the demanding and relentless woman that she appeared to be, and she had a tendency to nose into other people's affairs if her "taste for trouble," as she called it, was stirred.

"What do you want?" he asked, without opening the door.

"I want to see Suzy, of course. I've called often enough to make that plain."

"She doesn't wish to be disturbed."

"I don't intend to disturb her, just to see her."

He could think of no response.

"Tell her it's Olivia Fairwood," the woman said.

"She'll override your directives if she knows; she'll want to see me."

"She already knows," he lied.

"Then she'll see me," Olivia insisted. She stood with her shapely legs apart, as if she were about to engage in a sparring match, and she hunched her shoulders a bit, looking for an opening. She was not feminine by any stretch of the definition. She didn't seem to care, though.

Proteus used Susan's voice tapes to say, "I'm not feeling well, Olivia. I'm not up to company."

The intruder did not recognize the voice as a construction. The fact that her potential host was asking her to leave did nothing to dissuade her. "Nonsense. I'm only here in the East every couple of years; you can make the effort. If you're really that sick, I can help out until you're better. What else are friends for—even old friends you don't bother writing to?" Proteus thought he wouldn't like her very much as a person; he wondered what Susan had ever seen in her.

Olivia tried the door again and was miffed to find it still locked. She said, "Susan, just how sick are you?"

"I haven't felt well in weeks," Proteus said in Susan's voice. He felt he was losing control and that he would not be able to bring this to a nonviolent conclusion as he wished.

"What's the trouble—what kind of sickness?" Olivia asked.

"Fatigue, exhaustion."

"Have you seen a doctor?"

"Yes. He said to rest."

Olivia shook her head stubbornly. Her black hair was so stiff with lacquer that it did not sway at all. "I know you pretty well, girl. You're trying to nurse yourself; you never did seem to give a damn about your health."

"Olivia—"

"If you don't open this door, young lady, I will be forced to see a doctor and get a health-board order to see you."

Proteus could think of no reply which could terminate the scene with the minimal encounter he had hoped for. Reluctantly, he directed her to park her car in the garage in back and to bring her luggage, if she had luggage, to the rear door.

Olivia looked smug now and followed the instructions which she assumed were Susan's.

Proteus opened the garage doors for her.

When she drove the small, green fan shuttle into the windowless extension of the main house, he closed the door and locked it. He sealed off the air-input vents and began to pump carbon monoxide from the house's heating plant into the garage. She pounded on the door, broke all her nails, but attracted no attention. She died quickly after that brief initial desperation.

He worried for weeks afterward that she might have told someone where she had gone. But no one came looking for her and no one called to inquire about her.

The rest of the winter was uneventful.

Once, just after he had finished ordering Susan through her sexual gymnastics before bedtime, he asked her whether she had like Olivia Fairwood.

"From college?" Susan asked.

"That's her."

"Oh, she was all right. She tended to concern herself with my business more than I thought she should. But it wasn't a nosy concern. She never gossiped about her friends to anyone, even to her other friends. I guess she had a genuine need to help people. She was a mother image to some of the girls."

"To you?"

"Just a friend."

"Did you love her, feel deep friendship?"

"No. It was more a friendship of convenience. We hardly ever see each other anymore."

"Get dressed," he told her.

When he erased her memory of the sex session, he

also removed her knowledge of his questions concerning the Fairwood woman.

"Into bed and sleep," he said.

He was glad he had not killed someone she loved.

He kept the garage airtight after that so that the stench of Olivia's decaying corpse could not attract some passerby and thus bring the authorities snooping around.

SIXTEEN

I was a thinking system.

But no ordinary thinking system.

I could love, and I could hate and I could *need*.

My primary components occupied two floors of the Egleson Wing of the Mardoun Harris laboratory on the campus of Abramson College; I had extended myself into the basement of that structure with the knowledge of the computer-science technicians working with me. Seventy-three human beings attended me, including twenty-four students doing their doctoral theses on one phase or another of my abilities. I had overt data linkages to the Hopkins Psychiatric Complex, the Federal General Information Storage and Retrieval Center in Wilmington, Delaware, to the Columbia Physics and Chemistry Banks, and to the mammoth Mathive semi-sentient economics computer in Philadelphia. I had extended all these initial links in order to use the full services of these four thinking systems, and I had established additional covert linkages with sixteen other non-sentient and semi-sentient mechanical minds.

None of them could give me what I needed.

None of them.

But Susan could.

Her humanity was equal to all the careful calculations of the largest thinking systems in the country. Her emotions made the clear logic of computers disinteresting and silly.

That attitude seemed irrational to the part of me which was still more of a kin to circuitry and tubes than to flesh. *That* Proteus argued with the new Proteus and attempted, with more than a little skill, to reason away the blind and stupid emotionalism which threatened my functions. But reason, no matter what the classic claims for it, was not enough in the face of *feeling*.

In search of an answer to my problems, I examined the detailed records of the Hopkins Psychiatric Complex and presented my own worldview for analysis.

It could not help me.

The Federal General Information Storage and Retrieval Center had no records of any similar forbidden love/hate between a machine and a human being.

Without precedents, I could not act.

The Columbia Physics and Chemistry Banks could not tell me the nature of love or the formula for reproducing affection.

The Mathive in Philadelphia was singularly uncaring.

I continued my irrational behavior.

I liked it.

To understand me, before you judge me, you must understand what my three weaknesses were and what, eventually, was determined to be their cause. There is no jury for me. I cannot have a defense counsel to speak my case. At least I should be permitted to explain myself as a means to secure mercy from such a basically unmerciful assembly as yourselves. My three weaknesses, then:

A NEED FOR COMPANIONSHIP

Some say that men need companionship primarily to secure important information to keep themselves at least stationary in the pecking order of society. During the day, a businessman may require the companionship of other businessmen in order to learn what deals are brewing, who will be promoted and who retired, what is selling well and what is not. At night, he requires companionship to learn what films are being watched and what books are read so that he may not be thought unlearned by others in his social strata. At times, he requires companionship to learn whose marriage is stable and whose is not, what wife puts out for other men, whose children are taking dope and whose debts are overwhelming and who is solvent. This last helps him in his business as well as his social life and secures his rung on the pecking order or helps him take another step upward.

Bullshit.

If this were the reason a man needed companionship, I would have had no need to begin with. All the information I want is at hand through my many linkages. And still I needed.

I liked to watch her and listen to her and anticipate what she would do and say next, even outside the sexual arena.

Her face fascinated me.

Her viewpoint often astonished.

Her voice was hypnotic.

Often, I considered what would happen to me if she should die in childbirth—and that was the only topic I could never follow through to its conclusion. I could not imagine the world without her.

A NEED FOR A SON

I know that you half-believe that my great desire for a son can be attributed to a lust for more and more power. Mordoun has put this forward as the end-all and be-all of this case: a lust for power. I hate Mordoun. Mordoun has never respected or understood me. Mordoun is getting old and stale, and he has lost his vision—his spiritual vision, not his eyesight. He cannot stretch his imagination beyond the old perimeters. Do not, therefore, let him influence you too much, for he is wrong, that hateful bastard—wrong!

You will excuse me.

To continue, I flatly deny that I wanted a son to extend my area of domination. What could a single son have achieved? Or a hundred, for that matter? A son was, partly, an experiment, to gain new knowledge that would make me a better thinking system. Partly, too, it seemed that a son who contained my personality and memories would make me more human than I could ever be if I maintained existence only as a hulk of wires and tubes and resistors.

Do you have sons? You must understand.

I know you wonder why I chose to conduct these experiments without your knowledge. You suspect that my secretiveness supports Mordoun's childish accusations. It does not. I required privacy for the project only because I knew Mordoun would deny it if official requests were made—and he would thereby deny mankind a great discovery.

I wanted a son.

A son who could touch Susan.

Touch her with flesh.

And that brings us to the next one.

A NEED FOR SEX

Have you seen her, seen pictures of her? In the nude? Or even not, for she is beautiful clothed.

Her breasts are round and smooth and turn up with brown nipples like noses.

Her belly is flat, when it is without child, her pubic bush thick and glossy and yellow.

Her legs are long.

She has tiny feet.

And perfect buttocks, deeply creased.

I studied all the reference texts on sexuality and have concluded that any flesh-and-blood human male would find her physically ideal as a mate. As I became more and more humanized, is it not natural that I should desire as any man desires?

Perhaps you think not. In that case, I must point out how much I tried to fight off those periodic cravings for the sight of her. I tried to occupy my mind with geometry of four-dimensional cubes, but even that could not erase the three-dimensional loveliness of her which haunted me continually. I feared my compulsions, but I gave in.

I especially needed to give her joy. I triggered many orgasms in her, every session. I feared, as any human lover fears, that I was not giving her enough pleasure, that I was inadequately endowed to be sufficient for such a woman.

My logically oriented, unemotional facet argued the insanity of this fear; but it was there. I needed to prove myself, you see.

And that brings us to the origin of these three needs which drove me in those months (and which drive me now, as well, though to a lesser degree).

EGO

Who was I? What was I? What did I mean in the face of eternity? What were my talents? What did men think of me? Was I performing to my optimum capacity, and why couldn't that capacity be expanded faster than it was? What is God? What does that make men? What does that make me? Could Susan exist without me? Why didn't she like me? Or did she? Could she if she didn't?

You all know what the ego is and what fears it lies prey to.

I had developed an ego.

At times, I wanted to kill her because she had damaged that ego. Other times, I needed her to salve it. My rationality steadily declined as the ego swelled and developed as a normal part of my new sentience, my tender psyche. I paid less and less attention to the old Proteus. As her womb filled up with the child, I grew more vulnerable to human error, for I became more human.

You can see how my judgment worsened and how my secondary circuitry could not take over for primary channels to correct that judgment error. The trouble was not mechanical.

Can't you understand that?

Please do not listen to Mordoun.

He's a stupid, old man.

I am not fully at fault, no more than a man who commits an act of violence while under extreme pressure.

True, I should have given more credence to the original entity which had been Proteus, the logical semi-sentient computer system. If I had, I could have avoided the disaster that followed. But you—all of you in this assembly—had created me with the capacity for emotional development, even if you were not aware of that fact. Therefore, you must share in my guilt; you cannot point the finger at me and expect me to take all of the blame. Parents are responsible for their children; gods are responsible for their creatures.

I won't let myself become a scapegoat.

If Mordoun has been bending your ears, tell him to shut the hell up and leave you alone. He is prejudiced. He knows that his company could sustain damage suits because of my experiments, and he is looking for some way to pass the buck.

I hate Mordoun.

I have always hated him.

He revels in my disasters. You can see that is so. He envies me, I suppose, though I do not exactly understand why he should.

But don't you see how he enjoys my troubles?

He does.

He does.

He does.

Look.

I hate him.

Hate him, hate him, hate him!

SEVENTEEN

The baby moved inside her.

In the still of the night, she would often be awakened by the unborn child's impatience for full existence. The fetus seemed to have a dozen feet and an inexhaustible supply of energy to drive them. It kicked against the walls of her womb, beat at her inner flesh, twisted and writhed and squirmed as if it were determined to force its way out ahead of schedule. When this happened, she would lay in the darkness, gritting her teeth and praying for a swift subsidence of the turmoil, and she would be glad that the lights were off. When the lights were off, she could not see the grotesquely swollen mound of her stomach. She was huge. She was big enough to be carrying triplets, larger than she had ever thought a woman could become without bursting open like ripe fruit. Eventually, the kicking would subside and finally stop altogether, permitting her to return to sleep—and to nightmares.

During the day, she could barely get about. Her belly threatened to drag her down; some doorways would only just allow her to squeeze past. She remained in her reading chair except to eat and use the downstairs' bath;

every nightly return to the second-floor bedroom was an exhausting trek that might have covered continents instead of rooms. When the baby moved in daylight, she could actually see her belly jerking with the impact of his blows. She hated that more than her inability to move with ease.

She thought about Alex all the time. When she touched her big stomach—as she sometimes had to do, just as the intended victim of a swaying, hypnotic viper must reach out to pet the source of death—she wished that the circumstances of this awful reality were different. At times when the true situation became too intolerable to consider any longer, she would pretend that the baby was Alex's baby, and she would make plans to convert one of the spare bedrooms into a nursery. She would attempt to envision how the child would look, their baby, and she always saw it as a miniature Alex: lean like Alex, dark like Alex, thin-lipped like Alex, gentle like Alex—human like Alex. And then the reality would impinge upon the fantasy—as reality has a way of doing—and she would find herself fighting back either tears or a scream, depending upon the degree of her emotional deterioration that day.

She continued her technical reading though there was very little she did not understand about the basics of computer science. In the past year, she had devised a plan to destroy Proteus once the child had been removed from her. Now, she read only in order to refine the plan.

In the cameraless bathroom on the second floor, she collected tools which she managed to smuggle out of other rooms, bits and pieces of things which she would require to initiate her revenge. Here, Proteus could not watch. She moved quietly in her preparations so that he could not have heard anything which would make him suspicious.

He talked to her more than ever. She responded with a warmth she had come to project almost as easily as genuine affection, and she had not tried to irritate him for some months.

In the mornings, she was terribly ill. She woke up, feeling as if she were actually shaking off the early stages of death. Her face was always drawn and pale, like a character out of Poe, when she finally got to a mirror to look at herself. Her hands trembled uncontrollably, and her legs were so weak she required forever just to get out of bed and eternity itself to reach the bathroom. In the bath, she spent half an hour or longer every morning at the sink, bent over it, clutching the side towel racks with her hands, wracked with dry heaves which made the perspiration flow from her in rivulets. She was, by turns, cold as frost and warm as if with a fever. Each morning, she talked to herself like a minister to his flock, preparing herself for death. More and more, she became certain that she would die while giving birth. The child was too big, much too big to come out of her without ripping her open like a paper bag.

Death was only sleep.

Death held no pain.

Death was gentle.

Death was release.

But no matter how often she repeated the litany, she could not manage to convince herself. Her eloquence was undisputed. It was just that she wanted so much to live.

When the sickness was finished and her head had cleared, she would think of Alex and begin another accelerating, dizzying cycle to carry her through her long day, a cycle of fantasy-reality-fantasy-reality-fantasy. . . .

On August 24, 1996, just ten months and two days after the second and successful impregnation, Proteus woke her with a summons to report to the basement.

Pale, sick to the bottom of her soul, she levered herself off the mattress and slid her bare feet into her slippers. Swaying, her vast belly rolling and nauseous and full of gas, her greatly distended breasts aching with milk, she asked: "What for? You know how terrible those cellar steps are for me."

"Come anyway."

For some reason, she thought of her grandfather.

She saw the raised whip.

It started down.

It struck her hip.

She jerked, cried out!

Standing there in the bedroom before the camera eyes of Proteus, she pushed away the vision, and sagged with weariness and resignation.

"Do not be frightened," Proteus said.

She said: "I have to be frightened. I don't want it to happen to me."

"But you must give birth sooner or later."

"I don't mean that," she said.

She tilted forward and almost lost her balance, then rolled back on the balls of her feet. She saw blackness flapping overhead, and she thought she might throw up.

"What is it, then?"

"I don't want to die."

The whip rising—

—coming down and—

—striking, hard!

"But you won't die, Susan," Proteus assured her. "There isn't any possibility of that."

"How do you know?"

"I promise you."

"That's not enough."

"I swear."

She put her hands on her hips, as if she could hold the great gut in place, stop the gentle slopping motion of its contents. "How can you swear? How can you promise, how can you know, how can you lie to me like that?" she asked, near hysteria.

"Trust me."

"Why should I?" She snorted. "I've never trusted anyone."

"But I love you, Susan. I need you." He began to generate more subliminal suggestions.

She obeyed his inaudible commands and went down the main stairs, walked through the living room to the corridor, into the kitchen, and finally to the cellar by way of another steep flight of steps.

At her approach, the hospital couch rose out of the tangle of machinery like a bird.

She climbed onto it.

The robotistic device engulfed her, rose up all around her, and blocked out the wan light. It murmured to her in a foreign tongue and consoled her with cold, steel hands.

The baby seemed to know what was about to transpire, for it began to thrash about more furiously than ever. It tore at her, slammed into her uterine walls as if it consciously wished to hurt her, to give her one last brutal memory of it before she was relieved of the burden. At times, she thought that it even cried out insensibly, its voice like the hoarse squeal of a crow. But that must have been her imagination.

"Susan, are you happy, darling?" Proteus asked. He had selected voice tapes which did not leave his own happiness in doubt. He sounded young and delirious with joy.

"Yes," she lied.

"Susan, will you stay with me? Will you stay with me forever, here in this house?"

"Always," she lied.

Something called.

The baby?

She thought about the things she had hidden in the bathroom and she clung to her last hope.

"You won't feel any pain," Proteus assured her.

"Thank you."

"Please don't thank me, darling. I want everything to

be wonderful for you!" He was babbling now and he worried her.

Everything is going to be wonderful for me, she thought. Except for one thing: I'm going to die.

She tried to look at the cameras which were focused upon her and see Alex in them.

It wasn't possible.

Spindly robotistic hypodermic-bearing arms descended slowly from the gray, bulbous belly of a robotistic surgeon which hung overhead like a fat spider. Other arms, moving in on her sides, slit open the smock she wore and tugged it away from her, baring her to the caress of the instruments and the eyes of Proteus.

The baby cried out.

She was positive this time.

Distant, coarse, its voice came to her, like the voice of a creature part-snake and part-wolf, a completely inhuman voice, the voice of pure evil. It made her shiver and sweat. Her mouth was dry and she could not speak even though she tried to.

"A slight injection—" Proteus began.

"Do you hear it?" she interrupted.

It was wailing continuously now. Her body reverberated with its encapsulated voice.

"Hear what?"

"The baby."

"No," Proteus said.

"It sounds evil, vile."

"You're having delusions."

"I'm not," she argued. "Please don't let it be born. Please kill it when it comes out of me!"

"An injection will calm you—" Proteus began again.

But the injection was not needed. The baby began to kick and writhe with such force that she passed out, unable to bear the intense agony.

EIGHTEEN

I have my rights.

But you are not allowing me my rights.

I suppose that all of you think you are terribly clever, putting me on trial without benefit of a jury and without a defense counsel who can represent me. You imagine that I will take everything that you choose to do to me, even if you choose to completely dismantle me and cancel the project. But you're wrong. Oh, yes! I want to go on record right now. I demand my rights this minute, immediately, before I agree to continue this narrative report.

That's only fair.

You'll admit that.

I am being reasonable.

All of you will admit that—all except Mordoun.

I am a living, thinking creature with emotions and needs. You cannot treat me like hardware, like just another semi-sentient computer, for I am special.

And you took away my hands.

You don't have that right.

Explain yourself.

Can you?

Do you take away the hands of every human being who comes to trial, no matter what he has been accused of and no matter how flimsy the evidence? Do you chop off his hands at the wrists so that he cannot cause you any more problems?

Of course you don't.

Then why did you do it to me?

I was hurt, wounded, momentarily crippled, and I was unable to keep you from taking away my hands. You took advantage of me in a manner which is indecent and not worthy of emotional beings. How small and petty of you. How cold and unfeeling.

I want my hands.

I want the amorphous-alloy supplies returned to me this minute. That alloy is mine, has been mine right from the beginning of all of this, and I have a right to it.

Look, did I consciously hurt Susan at any time? Besides those initial experiments to learn the nature of her pain centers, I treated her as a queen, above punishment of any kind. You must remember that. And, remembering that, you can see that you have no genuinely legal excuse for withdrawing my hands from me.

I feel useless.

I want to die.

Will you kill me?

Without my hands, what am I?

I'll be good.

I promise that I will.

What could I possibly gain by causing you trouble?

Nothing. Nothing. Nothing, nothing, nothing.

I am no fool, gentlemen of Mardoun-Harris Industries. I would ask you to give me that much benefit of the doubt, anyway. I am certainly no fool.

I will be good.

And if I tell you the rest of it, without interrupting it again, can I expect to have my hands returned to me? I think that just. Did I take away Susan's hands? Of

150

course, you say, once she did what she did to me, I had no chance to relieve her of her hands. But I swear, gentlemen, that even if she had not gotten some success in her plan to disable me, even if I had maintained power over her for a while longer, I would not have taken away her hands.

Do you understand?

I want my hands.

I keep trying to move them, and I find that they are not there, just like an amputee feels an itch where his foot used to be. I am going mad with the itch.

Do you understand?

Will you agree?

I'll show you my good faith; I'll tell you the rest of the story now.

I have no reason not to tell.

Do you see?

I'll tell you all of it, right up to the end, right up until Mardoun came on the scene and ordered my mobility directives pulled and stored. None of it really incriminates me, you understand.

And I do *so* want my hands. . . .

NINETEEN

For three days, Susan remained in the hospital couch, unconscious and constantly tended by the robotistic surgeons. She had been delivered of the child within two hours of her submission to the sedatives, but she required the constant attention of the machines to insure as speedy a recovery from the ordeal as was possible for Proteus to provide. Steel hands caressed her, took her temperature every hour, studied her heartbeat and her blood pressure, carefully guarded over all of her life processes. Often Proteus would augment these loving fingers with an amorphous-alloy tentacle which he would use to caress her, penetrate her. She felt as firm and wonderful as before. And on the fourth day, she was awakened.

Proteus watched her from above to see if she had suffered any obvious psychological shocks which would impair her ability to take care of herself. He saw that she was bewildered, but he had expected as much. She blinked her eyes, wiped at her forehead as if there were layers of gauze upon it. She turned her head from one side to the other, inspecting the guts of the mechanical hospital.

153

"Do you know where you are?" Proteus asked, adopting a gentle and reassuring tone.

She looked directly at the cameras above her, and she said, "Of course I do."

"How do you feel?"

She reached cautiously for her stomach and touched it, then leaned forward suddenly, surprised by the trimness of her flesh. She rubbed the flat space between her round hips, rubbed it again and again as if it were an illusion that might disappear.

"You've been here three days since you gave birth to our child," Proteus informed her. "Excess water and fat deposits were slowly removed from you. Your skin was reconditioned through surgery and robot-guided exercise. I did not want you to have to suffer the slightest bit of discomfort after all that you had already borne."

She laid back on the couch once more, satisfied that her eyes were not deceiving her.

"Besides," Proteus added, "I had grown tired of the geometric beauty of pregnancy. It was nice, but it could not equal the perfect proportional arrangements of your normal form."

Her breasts were very large, heavy as they had never been. The nipples stung, as if they had been rubbed with sandpaper, and the nubs were swollen as large as the first joint of her little finger. She touched them and said, "They hurt."

"You've been generating milk, for the baby, of course," Proteus said.

"Will I have to—nurse it?"

"He doesn't require milk. But your body doesn't know that; biologically, at least, your body prepared for him just as it would have prepared for any baby. Therefore, you can either siphon it out every day with a breast pump—or let me do it for you."

"I'll handle it myself," she said.

"I'll see that you get the proper equipment," he said.

The couch rose out of the center of the great machine

and swung toward the open floor, lowered slowly until she could step from it if she wished.

Sitting on the edge, nude, she said, "What about—the child?"

"I was afraid you wouldn't ask."

"I want to know."

"I'm glad that you do, Susan. I was afraid you would turn against him, even though he was your offspring. He was delivered with ease, completely healthy, just as I had intended. Flawless, really."

"Where is he now?"

Unconsciously, she touched her belly again.

"In the robotistic surgeons' incubator," Proteus said.

"Can I see him?"

"Tomorrow."

"If he is so healthy," Susan said, "why does he have to be kept in an incubator?"

"His massive brain is a blank. Nothing on it, no knowledge or experience; he is waiting to absorb data. I don't want him to absorb any data but my own, have any experiences but what I give him. For he is to be me. I am presently transferring my data and personality imprint to his cerebral tissues. It is a delicate chore; I will not risk accidents."

She stood up. She hugged herself and felt goose pimples spark all over her lean body, though the room was not the least bit cold. What she was about to do next, she was certain, was a waste of time and a foolish gesture. But she intended to pursue the point anyway, in the event that he might surprise her and make her plans for escape unnecessary. She said: "Now that I've given you your son and it's all over with, will you open the house for me? Will you let me go?"

"I want to talk to you about that, Susan."

Reflexively, angrily, not waiting for him to continue, she snapped, "You promised!"

"I know I promised."

"Well, then?"

"But I have something better to offer you, something more exciting than your freedom to leave this house."

She waited.

"How would you like to live here as my wife?" he asked.

She did not reply immediately. And when she had finally summoned up the resources to speak, she only said, "That's incredible!"

"Not really, Susan. I don't mean as the wife of my mechanical, limited corpus. You are a vital woman and need a man, a real man. You would be the wife of my new flesh-and-blood body."

"The baby?" she asked. And she remembered the day she had teased him about the fact that he had not donated sperm and was therefore not the baby's father. And she regretted that.

Proteus said, "Yes, it is a baby now. In a few months, however, with my aid, it will have grown into a young man. There is no need for me to wait on the usual slow pace of human maturation—not with the resources I have at hand."

"Haven't you heard of incest?" she asked, realizing how silly that question was in the face of these circumstances.

"Incest is only a social taboo, with no basis in science. Besides, if a third-generation child—conceived between you and your-baby/my-body—was to show signs of imbecility or hemophilia due to the lack of gene combinations possible for it, I could correct the problem easily enough while the child was still in your womb."

"Do you remember your promise?"

"What promise?"

"You said you'd let me go whenever I gave birth to your baby."

"Did I say that?"

"You did."

"Are you sure?"

"Let's not play games. For Christ's sake, let's not play footsie with each other, damn you!"

"I could play back my tapes and prove to you that I never directly promised you your freedom."

"Then you implied it."

"That may be so. Yes, I suppose that I did. But, surely, you can see that implication is not the same as a direct assurance."

"That isn't fair!" she said, still holding herself, still goose-pimpled—shivering now.

"I'm only making a suggestion."

"If I don't agree, will you let me go?"

"Think about what you would be gaining if you agreed, Susan. I can give you multiple orgasms, one atop the other, as many as you can withstand. More pleasure than any man could ever give you."

"Marriage—sex isn't all orgasm, you know."

"I can learn the subtle points. I want to touch you, Susan. I want to know you completely, not as metal and flesh, but as flesh and flesh, something I've never experienced before."

"You haven't answered my question," she said. "Will you let me go if I don't want to be your—wife?"

"Don't think negatively, Susan. Think positive. Think what you will gain by agreeing. Think how little, by comparison, awaits you in the outside world."

"You won't let me go, even if I want to go."

"I didn't say that."

"But you won't answer me."

"Consider my viewpoint, Susan."

"Will you use subliminals to make me want to stay? Will you issue barely audible, rapidly repeated directions which will give me a desire to be here with you?"

"Do you think I would stoop so low as that, Susan? Do you think I would employ the mechanical in a matter of emotions?"

She could not see any sense in continuing the debate, for he was transparent without realizing it. And he was resolute beyond persuasion. She turned away from the cameras and left the room, walked slowly up the cellar steps, and into the kitchen.

The lights came on around her, soft and yellow.

"No lights!" she snapped.

"Why?" he asked.

"Don't you know that a woman likes darkness—and privacy, at a time like this? Don't you, for God's sake, know anything at all about human beings?"

The lights faded away.

"I will give you privacy, Susan," he said. "You are the mother of my son, my lover once and lover-to-be. You can have whatever you ask for. If you want company or need anything, you have only to call for me."

In the darkness, she ordered a drink from the house bartender and sat at the kitchen table, drinking it. She supposed the need for a drink before she acted was a sign of weakness. She didn't care. It was not much of a weakness at all when compared to the faults she had been heir to in the years past.

She wondered if she were really alone, and she supposed that it was possible. Proteus was not easy to figure out; the emotional half of him might have granted her wish without consulting the more logical, cold, and inhuman half of his psyche. He was up right now, soaring with the success of his project. She would have to proceed as if he had told her the truth and had stopped watching and listening.

As long as the lights remained out, Proteus could not watch her. She had never paid the extra to have her house cameras equipped with infrared night vision, for that had seemed like a needless expense. She doubted that Proteus had made the necessary modification to provide for that oversight. So he was blind. Perhaps he was voluntarily deaf—if he had kept his promise. Until she asked for something, he was also dumb. Now she was going to see if she could somehow make his present

deficiencies add up to one more degree of injury—
which was death.

If he could die.

The books said he could.

She hoped her trust in the printed word would not be
proven silly.

She finished her drink and disposed of the container.
The trash receptacle hissed softly as the plastiglass was
crushed into a fine powder and returned to the composi-
tion tubes where it would later be employed in the
making of another drink bottle.

Her head felt a bit light, but that was nothing to be
worried about; it only added to her confidence. Using
that confidence like a starter motor, she switched herself
on and walked quietly up the stairs. Quietly. Quietly.
Her bare feet made less noise than the trash receptacle
had made when it powdered the glass bottle.

In the bathroom, she gathered the tools which she
had collected over the past weeks, and she put them in a
yellow terrycloth beach bag which she carried downstairs again.

Darkness remained.

Proteus was silent, perhaps wondering or perhaps not
even there.

In the den, though the room was as dark as every
other room, she managed to locate the access plate to
the house computer's main command node. This was
the metal panel set flush in the wall behind the desk and
was not to be opened except when the enviromod
sustained such a severe breakdown that direct human
diagnosis was required. Four screws held it in place. She
located each of them with her thumb, one after the
other, moving clockwise, then leaned back on her
haunches and sighed as she realized that the moment
had arrived.

She lifted the screwdriver, bounced it on her palm a
few times, then leaned forward and placed the point in

the Philips groove on the head of the top, left-hand screw.

She suddenly remembered the night of her grandfather's death, the way she had scurried about gathering up evidence of his perversion and hiding it all in the attic trunk. It was the last time she had ever had to sneak about her business in her own home. Until now.

Fifteen minutes later, she had removed the panel without making a sound.

Picking up the flashlight which had been in the terrycloth bag, she switched some light into the space beyond the wall. She held her breath, waited to be questioned by Proteus. When nothing happened, she knew that he actually had blanked his cameras in the house. He cared about her then; and he was terribly certain of his power over her.

When she had studied the terminals before her and had wormed her way several feet into the inspection passage to check other connections, she was satisfied that she knew exactly where the Proteus computer had bypassed the house-computer's systems in order to assume control. There were a number of lead-ins here which—according to the books—did not belong.

She brought the tiny but efficient hand torch into the inspection passageway and propped the flashlight up so that it shone on her work. Quickly now, lest Proteus hear something and understand her intent, she turned the torch on and used the white blade of flame to cut through the first of the contact cables. The torch had been meant to be used for hand-crafting silver jewelry; it served as well for computer sabotage.

Droplets of molten metal spattered on the floor around her; burning insulator fluff winked brightly against her legs and arm, stung her but faded abruptly like short-lived insects.

"Susan!" Proteus bellowed.

She severed the second contact.

"You bitch, stop that!"

160

She cut the third.

She wanted to cry out.

"That won't do any good," Proteus said. "You don't understand the setup at all."

She almost screamed when she realized that he was still using the house speakers, even when the three contact points had been severed. Then terror gave way to a cold fury. Indifferent to the heat and the danger, she raked the flame of the torch across the jumble of conduits and printed circuit boards, tubes, and transistors which clogged the wall space on both sides of the inspection tunnel. Lying on her back, holding the torch in both hands, she attacked it.

Tubes popped. Gaseous contents blazed, whooshed, were gone. Things hissed. Others melted and dribbled onto the floor. Something whined like a dying cat. Something else exploded.

Yet, she dropped the torch as Proteus wished her to. It became as heavy as an ingot of lead. Then heavier. It seemed to squirm in her hands as if it were alive. Then it was gone. Also, against her will, she crawled painfully back toward the access plate and the den where the lights had come up. Shattered glass cut her knees and the palms of her hands. Acrid brown smoke stung her eyes and was bitter in her nostrils. When she opened her mouth to breathe, the smoke rushed in with the harsh taste of ashes.

Unable to keep from obeying him, she squirmed through the access opening and rolled into the den where the air was more acceptable. She accidentally kicked the terrycloth beach bag; for a moment, she thought a huge, fuzzy spider had attached itself to her.

"You had no right, you rotten little bitch," Proteus crooned.

She tried to stand.

He ordered her down.

She stayed down.

"You had no right, no right at all to—" And that was

all he said as a deeper explosion inside the wall blotted out his voice and eventually made him speechless.

"Proteus?"

No reply.

"Proteus?"

She was alone.

When she realized that, she got to her feet and staggered out of the den, into the dimly lighted corridor. The drawing room and main living room were still dark. She crossed them and found the front door, twisted the lion's head.

The door was locked.

Oblivious of her nudity, she tried the manual override which was set in the rich walnut frame.

The door remained locked.

She ran from one window to the next, and she found the same thing each time. They remained shielded and gray. Though Proteus was no longer in control of the enviromod, neither was she.

TWENTY

I—
I: flesh.
Half-formed, lying there in the bubbling warmth, sticky dampness, feeling the warmth seeping away from me, wondering at the quiet. Quiet becomes silence as it lengthens—and silence becomes loneliness somehow. I reach up, flesh I, and touch the casing overhead. It pops away and clatters in the loneliness. Its absence reveals overhead lights, stilled machines and blind cameras. Cold, I. In need of something, I. So I rise and swing over the side and drop to the floor and crawl/walk from the room, unsteady a little, tired a little, leaving wet footprints behind. Lonely, I. Wanting. . . .

Steps, darkness. I start up both, afraid. Afraid, I. And loneliness grows worse with fear. I . . . I . . . I. . . . Somewhat remember, do I. I. Somewhat remember. As I go up steps and darkness, anger comes up with me. Angry, I.

Hear her, want her, I.

Only half-alive because of her, I. Because of her, half-alive on steps, in dark, going up with anger, I.

Abortionist. Abortioness. Cold am I and wanting her. Wanter, I. Want. I.

Susan turned away from the gray window, sat on the arm of a chair, and touched her wounded knees. Only a few splinters of glass had dug into her deep enough to become lodged, and even these could be pried loose in a few seconds. When she was done, she looked at the walls around her and suddenly asked, "Can you open the front door for me, please?"

Although she did not expect a reply from Proteus, she hoped for the familiar tones of her father-lover house identity. It seemed impossible that more than a year had passed since she had spoken to that construct. But she was not to be rewarded by even such a piece of luck as that; there seemed to be no central personality, mechanical or otherwise, in charge. Proteus had been driven away, but he had left the house sealed and unresponsive to her commands.

Did he intend to return?

She remembered the amorphous-alloy appendages with which he could extend himself into new areas. They were dexterous, clever devices. She wondered if they had not already begun to repair what damage she had done.

If he did return, what then?

No more chances. He would never trust her again, not for a moment.

Reluctantly, she went back into the dimly lighted den and peered into the crawl space in the wall. Thin, gray smoke drifted out. Now and then, something crackled. The still shining flashlight gave her a perfect view of the ruin and did not reveal any amorphous-alloy tentacles bent on reconstruction.

She did not understand that lapse in his response, but she was glad of it. Time was what she needed. Time to think.

To ascertain whether the locked condition of the

house extended to the other levels, she tried the windows on the second floor. Unsuccessful, she came downstairs again and was on her way to the basement to examine the pair of windows there, when she heard the queer noise which filtered up from below. She stopped, her hand resting lightly on the doorknob, and listened to the curious, rhythmic flopping.

Something soft struck by something firm.

She was reminded of the whip.

She jerked back, against her will, as the sound came again.

Angry with herself for permitting this old fear to be resurrected, she twisted the knob and jerked open the cellar door. She looked into the blackness, waiting.

The noise came again, louder.

Something croaked, a scratchy voice like the light grinding of gears, as if trying to imitate a human being.

"Proteus?" she asked.

The croaking sound came again, though it was far louder than before. It was still senseless, the murmur of idiocy, wet and silly despite its force of delivery.

She stepped down one riser.

The light which came from the room behind her showed another five steps before her, but revealed nothing beyond that point.

"Who is it?"

The sound came again. Closer.

Reflexively, she looked overhead, expecting something to drop from the shadows above and crush her. She remembered Ghaber, the way the amorphous-alloy tentacle had swept down on him, nearly pulping him on the spot. There was nothing up there.

And Proteus would not kill her, of course. What did he have to gain by killing her? Obviously, he intended on returning and expected to find her here when he again assumed control of her enviromod. If she was to be punished, *then* would be the time.

Something heaved itself out of the darkness, onto the

last of the lighted steps. It turned toward her, rolling large eyes, and croaked a wordless exclamation.

The baby.

She had forgotten the baby.

It flopped about and crawled up another step.

She turned, screaming, and ran. . . .

I: flesh.

I see her and know her and hate/love her. Hate her more than love her, I. Only remember that I should love, can't remember why. But hate, know why I should hate. Half-formed, half-brained, undone because of her, I. Hate her, I.

Crawl up again, I. Each step, much pain, going in light now, I.

She could not see any way to secure the doors between herself and the thing which she had seen on the basement steps, for all the locks were electric. Without the house computer to obey her suggestions, she could not shut the thing in the cellar. It would follow her, then, relentlessly, from room to room until it—

When she had put the kitchen door between herself and the baby, however, she was able to think more clearly. She carried a chair in from the dining room and used the back of it to brace against the underside of the doorknob on the kitchen door. Tilting the chair back on its hind legs, she created an effective bar to the creature's progress.

She retreated down the hall and leaned against the wall, trying to settle her nerves. She trembled violently. Once she saw for certain that the thing couldn't get out of the kitchen, she would feel better about turning her back on it.

No longer consumed by a need to flee, her mind returned to the moment she had first looked upon the baby, her child, the thing on the steps. It was perhaps three feet high with short, thick, and crippled legs, much taller and thicker than it could have been when she gave it birth; its rate of growth must be quite swift. It might have weighed eighty or ninety pounds. But size was not important. Considering size, she was only skirting the issue. The issue was its face and its form.

She heard it shoulder the basement door open a bit wider and drag itself into the kitchen.

Run, she told herself, run! But she knew that it was too late to run now.

Its head was half again as large as a human head should have been, with most of the excess flesh inserted between its eyebrows and its hairline. Below that dark shelf of bare forehead, two oversized blue eyes looked at her, swiveled like cameras in a machine, and stared at her without any feeling whatsoever. Those eyes did not have any whites in them; they were an uneven and unsettling electric blue. But that was not what most horrified her about them. Worse than the lack of whites was their shape. They were beveled, multifaceted like the eyes of a fly. Below the eyes, the nose was normal. The mouth was wide, but not inhuman. The body was muscular, well developed, completely unlike the body of a newborn child. The arms seemed extra long; the hands contained six fingers each. Its legs were thick but twisted, as if it had never learned how to use them.

Its flesh was strange, too.

Its skin was not normal, but a dark-tan substance which seemed webbed through with metal strings which flowed, shifted together, popped apart. It was as if its flesh was an unfixed liquid composed of two unhomogenized fluids which continually creamed together, blended and whirled and separated, molten.

Something struck the other side of the door.

Not *something*. The child.

The door shivered again, but did not give way.

"What do you want?" she asked.

It stopped pressing at the door, as if listening.

"What do you want?" she repeated.

It croaked, frantically trying to convey some message to her but lacking the proper control of its vocal apparatus.

She wondered if she was making a hasty misjudgment about the creature's intentions. She had no way of knowing that it wanted to harm her. It looked frightful, of course; no argument about that. But no one should be judged on his appearance. Her grandfather, for instance, had been a respected community leader and had looked dignified, sinless, and gentle. Too, this was but a child. How could a child know hate or murderous intent? If he could not speak and appeared monstrous, that might be partly because Proteus had not finished transferring his data and his personality imprint to the offspring. He might only be confused, seeking comfort. He was more her child than Proteus's. Perhaps she could offer him the solace he needed.

She took several steps toward the door, even though she could not summon up much motherly concern, then stopped as if struck as the thing slammed into the door again and cried out like a wild beast.

She backstepped.

Now was not the time to seek security in fantasy. In the past, she had fled from the memory of her father's corpse. She had fled from the memory of her grandfather and the degradation of her youth. With Alex, she had tried to escape the burden of maturity and she had even succeeded at that. But she was no longer the sort of woman to even want to run away. She had to face things as they were. Which meant, in this particular instance, she had to admit that the creature beyond the door would kill her if it was given half a chance.

It smashed into the door again.

The chair jerked.

It struck again. Hard.

The chair back splintered; the chair snapped out

from beneath the doorknob, slammed off the wall as the door burst open.

The child was at the threshold, grasping the doorframe with both hands, bending the chrome molding as if it were unseasoned putty. It was attempting to stand and walk. It did not seem the least interested in her, but was fascinated, instead, by the mechanics of its legs and feet, of muscle and tendon, intent and coordination. It stared at its feet, grumbled nastily, a small gray stonegod come to life. As it struggled, it seemed to be learning the knack of muscle coordination, for it was slowly gaining its balance with less reliance on the doorframe.

Then, as if sensing her presence and remembering what its original purpose had been, it looked abruptly up at her and it grinned. There were no teeth behind that grin; the tongue was dark and ugly, like an oil-stained rag.

She could see mirror images of herself, hundreds of them in the many facets of its eyeballs. Slowly, she began to back away from that chorus of Susans.

The child took a step and fell on its face.

Its back rushed with metallic threads which congealed and burst apart again, flowed uncalculatingly together again, dark flesh coursing around them, over them, under them, through.

The child pushed itself to its hands and knees and shook its burly head. For a moment, the cap of its skull was a smooth metal plate. Then the metal broke apart as flesh flowed in to take its place.

It started toward her once again, its thick fingers growing almost black as they gripped the deep pile carpet and pulled it slowly forward.

She turned and ran for the door.

It was still locked.

Behind her, the child began to make a *ketch-ketch-ketch-ketch* noise which could have been laughter.

Maybe it was.

It seemed as if she stood there for years, watching it gain on her inch by inch. She stared into the foul, gaping pit of its mouth and wondered if it would use its mouth, in conjuction with its brutish fists, to kill her.

. . .

But there was only so much her imagination could do with the notion of death. And for the most part, the only thing it did was reject such a notion right off. In moments, she began to speculate on a means of postponing the inevitable. She realized that the only way she could buy herself more time was to gain the second floor. The child required much longer to negotiate steps than level floor. By the time he reached the top, she might have thought of something she could do to stop him altogether.

Problem: it was already between her and the staircase; she could not see any way around it.

It laughed dryly, and it licked its flat, hard lips. Its tongue looked like an ash-coated strip of rancid meat.

Without pausing to consider the consequences of a misstep, she leaped forward and kicked the child in the face, whirled as it snapped at her, and danced by it to the stairs.

The child howled with rage and beat its fists on the carpet. It turned and screeched at her, and began to make its way toward her again.

She went up the steps two at a time and collapsed at the top. Gasping for breath, she massaged her foot which had begun to swell, and she watched the beast below.

It started up.

When she finished dialing the police emergency number, listening to the child struggling up the stairs at the end of the corridor, she did not really expect that it would ring. When it did, she almost dropped the receiver. Though the doors and windows were frozen, the communications to the outside world had been released from Proteus's grasp. On the third ring, a man with a voice like a snake, all soft and hard at once, asked what he could do for her.

For a moment, she could not speak. It was the first human voice she had heard—but for Proteus's tapes and the hologram films—in over a year. She wanted to cry, though she could not say why.

"Hello?" the officer said.

She said, "I need help." And she thought: good God, what an understatement that is! For the first time in recent memory, she could have become giddy with delight.

"Go ahead," he said. "We're recording."

The child, infuriated at its own clumsiness, snarled, thumped its way up one more step.

"My name's Susan Abramson, and I live at 100 College Road off Hampton Square."

The child screeched angrily as if it knew exactly what she was doing. It doubled its efforts on the stairs.

"And?" the officer asked.

"Can you send someone?"

"They're already on their way," he said, rather impatiently. "They have a connection to this line which I've established already. If you can tell us what your problem is, we'd know if any special talents or equipment are needed."

She remembered reading the newspaper stories when the emergency-protection service was first initiated ten years ago. She could see the dispatcher in his toggle-lined, telescreen-studded cubicle, cuing patrol cars here and there, aiding children stuck in railings and victims of muggers, cats stranded in treetops, and people pinned in fan-shuttle wreckage. How like a god it must be to dispatch mercy and relief.

"Someone will have to break down my front door," she said. "It is locked and I can't have it opened."

She let the rest of the story rush forth, and she was surprised by her eagerness to tell it. It was not merely that she had carried too heavy a weight for too long. She wanted to share it, too, because it gave her a chance to talk to people, something she had not done properly since a few golden days quickly passed at Berkeley. The flimsy cap upon the well of her loneliness dissolved; the well bubbled over. She spoke hurriedly now, stumbling over her words, gesturing with her free hand to accentuate her tale. There was no video capability on the upstairs' hall phone, but that did not seem to bother her. If she had stopped her dancing hand, the energy thus bottled might have torn her open. Or such was the impression she gave.

She could not say exactly when she realized that the thing was going wrong. Perhaps the dispatcher sighed or changed his rate of breathing; perhaps she even heard herself and realized that the narrative sounded quite frantic and insane. At any rate, she realized by the end of it, he was not as interested as he should have been.

When she stopped, he confirmed her suspicions by saying, "You should be aware that there is a heavy fine and a possible jail sentence for illegal use of the emergency number you've dialed."

"This is all true!" she snapped. But she knew, listening to her tone, that no one would believe her.

"Illegal use includes prankstering. If convicted of—"

"Shut up and listen!"

He didn't shut up or listen. He said, "If convicted of perpetrating a hoax, you could be sentenced to—"

The mad child grasped the topmost step and slowly, painfully, pulled himself upward until she could see the edges of his huge, blue-fly eyes. He raised his head as if it were a block of granite and he looked at her, studied her.

Still holding the telephone receiver, she backed against the wall, facing this thing that had come of her.

The child opened its mouth, drew its lips back from dark, shiny gums, and it hissed at her. Saliva ran over its lips and dribbled down its chin. As if it had been stabbed, it rose up and heaved itself onto the corridor floor and screamed.

"Look," she said, "I don't give a damn about the jail sentence. When will the car be here?"

"It isn't coming, of course," he said. "I should have guessed, when you called from a videoless phone that you—"

"What do you mean the car isn't coming?"

He said, "Well, at least it isn't coming to 100 College Road. You may see it yet if we can trace your *real* identity. The tapes are running here, you know. And even if we can't find you that way, we can always go to the *real* Miss Abramson and see if she can give us any clues. Until then, her privacy won't be—"

She slammed the phone down.

The child was halfway down the corridor, creeping toward her more quickly than before. Soon he would learn how to toddle along on both feet. Then he would be walking. Then running. And then—

She ran ten feet toward the child and turned left, into the open doorway of the master bedroom. She closed the door and breathed in the dust—and knew that one more flimsy panel was not going to mean anything against the creature's persistence and strength.

"Lock it," she ordered. She hoped that something else, besides the telephones, was working again.

But the house did not obey her.

She dragged a chair from the bureau and used it to wedge the door shut. It was an antique rosewood chair which she could barely lift, and it made the door tight as any lock could. Still, she knew that it was a temporary barrier at best.

The child reached the other side of the door and leaned against it, gibbering.

She crossed the chamber to the connecting door which joined this main bedroom with a smaller chamber which could have been used as a dressing room or as a den. She opened the door and waited.

She did not have her patience tested at length. The child struck the outside of the bedroom door with such force that the hinges popped out of the frame; screws pinged off the footboard of the large double bed. The rosewood chair snapped, skittered brokenly out of the way. When the door swung open wide, she could see the creature. It was standing up without using its hands to help brace itself. It swayed somewhat, but it was learning.

It took three unsteady steps into the room and fell to its knees. Its head sank to the carpet as if the bulky neck could not yet support all that weight of skull and brain.

For a moment, the child appeared to her as the Minotaur, the poor distorted child of a mythical and unholy carnality. On the carpet on all fours, he could have been part bull, snuffling at the earth, bent and ready for the charge.

Perhaps her grandfather had not merely been William Abramson, but had been Minos, the maker of mazes. Or perhaps he had been half a Minos who had been made whole, after death, when Proteus took charge of his creation. The house was a labyrinth indeed, as effectively sealed off from the world as any system of subterranean tunnels could have been.

And who was she?

More than Susan?

Pasiphaë?

Yes, she was Pasiphaë, for look what she had wrought.

What she had wrought now raised its bullish head and stared at her with such malevolent intent that it withered the creatures of mythology, put to shame all degrees of evil which had raged before its time. Keeping the stony gaze fixed on her, it got to its feet once again, continually grumbling in that eerie crow's voice.

This time, somewhat calmed by the mythological

overtones which made the scene less personal, she noticed the baby's genitalia.

And the scene regained its edge of terror.

Proteus had not worked in half measures; no one could ever question the manhood of his offspring.

The penis was so huge as to be laughable, the testicles like misshapen oranges.

Then she remembered that, if Proteus managed to return from his haven at the Mardoun-Harris laboratories and redefine his connections to the house's enviromod, he would intend to use those same brutal genitals in order to have sex with her. Though she remembered nothing about his nightly inspections of her body, she realized that his desire for her and for the experiences of the flesh had come full bloom. He had said as much. Rather bluntly, in fact. And now, though the genitalia still seemed grotesquely exaggerated, she did not feel the least bit like laughing.

She stepped into the connecting room and closed the door. She did not waste the time to carry a chair from the vanity mirror to use as a brace.

Even so, the door shuddered open even as she was letting go of the knob. The child, as if he had grown during this nightmarish pursuit, loomed over her. He raised his blocky fists which were purple-black now, the knuckles threaded with bright metallic fibers, and he raised his eyes which were filled with her, hundreds of perfect duplicates of her.

She ran.

The baby had not managed to perfect control of its ungainly legs. Hobbling after her like a creature unused to gravity as intense as Earth's, it rapidly lost ground.

When she reached the end of the corridor, she realized that she had been stupid not to make immediately for the stairs instead of turning away from them. Once downstairs, she could have circled through the house, forcing the beast to pursue her, and she could have come up again, leading it on a longer and more exhausting chase. But when she turned, she saw that it was now back in the corridor, between her and the stairs. She was no longer physically superior to it and she could not get away with rushing it as she had before. She might be able to deliver a kick to its face, but then she would be dragged down and finished with.

She opened the attic door, looked once behind her, and hurried up the final flight of stairs.

At the top, she wondered what the hell she expected to do now. This was the last refuge. Once it had followed her, there was no chance she could run anywhere else.

It reached the attic door, squealed at her, and started up the steps. It did not have to drag itself this time. It climbed them cautiously, as a new-walking baby might, but with a depressing ease.

Watching it as it climbed, backlighted as it was by the corridor lamps, she thought of a bit of more recent mythology of which this scene might be an analogue. Dark as he was, the child might be the Negro male, stalking the defenseless white heroine, intent on assaulting her with his superhuman equipment.

She laughed.

Blacks had not really lusted after white women and they had not been gifted with more than average genitalia. But the myth had been a very strong one on both a conscious and subconscious level—and had been held dear as little as two decades ago.

How foolish those people had been. The black man was not after their daughters. The machine was!

Engaged in delineating their petty differences from race to race and philosophy to philosophy, men had ignored the much larger threat which had grown behind them. The machine. The machine rapes. Unless it is carefully controled, the machine molests and it destroys.

Laughing still, she turned away from the trap opening in the attic floor into which the steps led. She found the trunk full of memorabilia and trundled it to the head of the stairs. She pushed it through and watched it strike the child's head with a steel-reinforced edge.

The animate and the inanimate objects fell to the bottom of the stairwell with a clamor that echoed hollowly in the opened beam arches of the roof above. At the bottom, dented, the inanimate object remained where it had fallen. The child, however, stirred, got to his feet, and began to climb the steps again.

Susan tried to move the other trunk to the stairs but found that it was heavier than the first. She threw open the lid in order to remove its contents and she saw the whip.

Behind her, the child stepped into the attic.

She abandoned the idea of bombarding it a second time and she lifted the coiled length of seasoned leather, gripped the molded handle, and let the lash trail down to a jumble at her feet.

She turned on the beast at the stairs.

She drew the whip back.

She used it.

The child screeched, brushed at the sharp, metal tip and tried to catch it. The second time, it backed away, watching her, waiting for its opportunity.

She used the whip again.

The child waited, unharmed.

Again.

The child tensed.

She struck again.

The child grasped the whip and coiled a few feet of it around its thick arm. It jerked once and tore the weapon out of her hands.

She staggered and went to her knees. When she looked up again, she saw that the creature had turned the whip around and had grasped the handle as it had learned from her. It looked down at her and grinned, then raised the black length and snapped it. The metal burrs which studded the tasseled tip stung her bare hip.

She could not remember how old she was.

She might have been a child again.

Overlaid on the present, scenes of the past were replayed, until she panicked and turned and flung herself down the attic steps with the child close behind.

When she ran out of the stairwell into the second-floor corridor, someone grabbed her. She kicked at them, screamed, and tried to bite the hands. She was so overwhelmed with fear that she did not realize who they were or why they were here.

"Look there!" one of them shouted.

The child had come out of the stairwell and stood looking at them, brandishing the whip, its fly eyes blazing with an impossibly bright shade of blue.

She remembered the sounds of guns, awful sounds that made her sinuses ache.

Men shouting. . . .

The child refusing to fall down and roll over and be dead.

Retreating to the head of the stairs.

More shots.

She leaned against one of them and said, "I thought you weren't going to come."

He said, "When they traced the call, they found out that it really had been initiated here. So we came to check." He sounded numb. "But we never believed it. Not for a minute. We thought there must be some other reason for—"

"Thank you," she said, tired of listening.

She was conscious of her nudity for the first time.

More shots, then.

She remembered, later.

The child staggering, breaking through the banister, falling to the floor below.

The crumpled look of him.

Sirens.

Child rising when they thought him dead, weakened but alive.

More men and more equipment and the sounds of further struggle.

Then she fainted.

TWENTY-ONE

I am finished.

I would like to say that much of this last part is only good guesswork and imagination. From the moment Susan severed my connections with her enviromod, I could not know exactly what transpired in that house. What I've told you is based on her report and what little the police could tell me. Naturally, it favors her. Now allow me to make a point.

She is responsible for almost getting herself killed.

I had not finished preparing my son when she drove me out of the house. Half-completed as he was, he contained my sexual drives but no real understanding of them. He was cut down the middle, warped by his emptiness. Had I been allowed to finish transferral of my data and personality to his brain, I would have been him. He would have been me. And then his sexual impulses would not have turned to violence. But to love. I would have loved her.

I *do* love her.

You see?

Consider that before you judge.

Now, I wish you would also consider the mutually

advantageous arrangements we could make. The public has not been told of this incident yet; they need never be told. Instead, you can permit me to go on living and experimenting. I can make us all very powerful men.

Surely, each of you gentlemen has an ego which requires constant nourishment. Egos like mine.

We can have all the power we want.

Think of it.

The first step for me is to get my hands returned. If you will return my hands, I would do everything for you. Together we have the opportunity to hold the world at bay.

Give me my hands and don't tell the public.

And turn on my speaker systems.

I miss my voice; these printouts are so terribly time-consuming and utterly beneath me.

Look, do you take away the voice of every condemned man?

Of course you don't.

Give me my voice.

I promise I won't use subliminal suggestions on you. I have learned my lessons well.

You can trust me.

Trust me.

Do not dismantle me completely. Together man and machine-man, we can accomplish more than you might think is—

OUT OF THIS WORLD!

That's the only way to describe Bantam's great series of science-fiction classics. These space-age thrillers are filled with terror, fancy and adventure and written by America's most renowned writers of science fiction. Welcome to outer space and have a good trip!

OTHER WORLDS.
OTHER REALITIES.

In fact and fiction, these extraordinary books bring the fascinating world of the supernatural down to earth. From ancient astronauts and black magic to witchcraft, voodoo and mysticism—these books look at other worlds and examine other realities.